He smiled an[...] the dance floo[...] into an intima[...] smooth musk scent of his cologne filled her [se]nses as she pressed her body into his muscu[la]r frame. She wrapped her arms around his [n]eck, resting her head on his shoulder. His arms circled her waist, one resting just above her [re]ar as he held her close. They moved to the music, allowing the smooth rhythm to flow over [the]m. A sense of belonging washed over her. He [felt] right, too right. He was starting to evoke feel[ings] within her that scared her. His hand ca[ress]ed her back, molding her into him. She [clos]ed her eyes, giving in to the safe, soothing [feel] of him. His hand moved up to caress the [bac]k of her neck. He gently pulled her head off [his] shoulders. She gazed at him, opening her [eye]s. The look in his eyes took her breath away. [He] wanted her and it was all there in his eyes. [The] blatant knowledge of it sent shivers down [her] spine. Kelee couldn't deny the fact that she [wan]ted him, too. Her heart raced at the thought, [the] possibility of being with him in the most in[ti]mate way. He lowered his head to hers and [Ke]lee closed her eyes as his lips covered hers in [a s]low heated kiss.

This Time

INGRID MONIQUE

Dafina Books

Kensington Publishing Corp.

http://www.kensingtonbooks.com

DAFINA BOOKS are published by

Kensington Publishing Corp.
850 Third Avenue
New York, NY 10022

Copyright © 2006 by Ingrid Monique Green

All Kensington Titles, Imprints, and Distributed Lines are
available at special quantity discounts for bulk purchases
for sales promotions, premiums, fund-raising, and educa-
tional or institutional use. Special book excerpts or cus-
tomized printings can also be created to fit specific needs. For
details, write or phone the office of the Kensington special
sales manager: Kensington Publishing Corp., 850 Third
Avenue, New York, NY 10022, attn: Special Sales Department,
Phone: 1-800-221-2647.

Dafina and the Dafina logo Reg. U.S. Pat. & TM Off.

First Dafina mass market printing: May 2006

10 9 8 7 6 5 4 3 2 1

Printed in the United States of America

_This
Time_

Chapter 1

Kelee Kingsly stepped from the plane and was greeted by the brilliant St. Pala sun, which instantly warmed her body. She slipped on her shades as she descended the stairs of the plane. The heat was welcoming compared to the thirty-degree chilly weather she left in Manhattan, New York, three hours ago. She stepped down onto the hot black tarmac. The intense heat made her skin tingle, causing beads of sweat to form on her upper lip. It was a little after one P.M., the hottest time of day. A cool breeze coming off the ocean whipped at her shirt, making the heat bearable. The scent of raw sea breeze mixed with jet fuel invaded her nostrils, bringing back memories of her native Jamaica. St. Pala wasn't much different from Jamaica; they both had great people, food and weather. No matter which Caribbean island Kelee visited, she always felt like she was coming home once she stepped foot on the hot tarmac.

Kelee made her way towards the entrance of the arrival building along with her fellow passengers, who consisted of natives and tourists. Inside the cool terminal Kelee made her way through a sea of natives and tourists to baggage claim. Fifteen minutes later she saw her four large suitcases coming around on the conveyor belt. Kelee always overpacked, it was just her style. She tended to change clothes a lot depending on her mood. She was only going to be in St. Pala for a few months, or until her niece was born.

Kelee was struggling to get her first bag off the belt when a young man was kind enough to help her unload her cases onto a cart. She thanked him, and made her way towards customs. She frowned at the sight of the long lines. She hated the wait that came with exiting customs, and from the look of the lines she knew it would be another thirty minutes before she could exit the barely cool airport.

"Kelee." She heard her sister's voice. Kelee scanned the mixture of multicultural faces for her sister's. She heard her name again and followed the voice. She spotted Lori waving her over to the far end of the customs desks. She smiled and waved back, excited. Kelee hadn't seen her sister in three years. She maneuvered her cart through the crowd, focused on her sister.

Lori was the taller of the two at five ten. Kelee was a mere five three and had always envied her sister's height. They both had their father's cool bronze coloring, but had inherited their mother's long thick hair. They also had their mother's light brown eyes, accentuated by high cheekbones, small round noses, and full lips. The resemblance between them was uncanny. Unlike her sister, who wore her hair in natural twists, Kelee wore hers bone straight, falling down the middle of her back.

Kelee's eyes fell to Lori's protruding belly and she squealed in joy. She hugged and kissed Lori. It was so good to see her big sister; she had missed her so much. The sisters held on to each other for what seem like a lifetime. Kelee rubbed Lori's belly, smiling. She couldn't wait to be an aunt.

"I can't believe yu' here," Lori exclaimed, tearing up. Kelee hugged Lori again, taking in her fresh floral scent. It felt good to be close to her.

"I'm glad to be here," Kelee responded.

"Yu' are stayin' until the baby's born?" Lori asked with a stern look.

"Yu' know I will." Kelee smiled and kissed her cheek.

A huge smiled consumed Lori's face. "Good, because I need yu'."

"Yu' got me."

"Ladies." A customs officer walked over to them. He was tall and thin with a ready smile.

"She's with me," Lori told the officer and he nodded, offering his assistance by pushing Kelee's cart towards the exit. Kelee was thankful she wouldn't be searched. Getting through customs without the hassle of being searched was one of the perks that came with being married to the minister of tourism of St. Pala, which Lori's husband was. Lori was well known on the island, for her high-profile community activities.

The receiving area outside was filled with people awaiting visitors and family. Lori's driver waited for them by a large SUV jeep. Kelee helped her sister into the middle seat, joining her as the driver collapsed the backseat and loaded up her cases. The sisters held hands, catching up as they made their way to Lori's home on Rose Hill. Rose Hill was one of St. Pala's upscale neighborhoods, overlooking the splendor of the city of St. Pala below. Kelee had always loved the view of rolling hills and city nested in the valley. The last time she was in St. Pala was four years ago, for Lori's twenty-fifth birthday party. This time she was here for the birth of her niece.

"Mom called this mornin'; she wants yu' to call her," Lori told her. "She said she hasn't heard from yu' in months." They were on the back veranda overlooking the pool, sipping iced teas.

"I know. I hope she's not too mad at me." Kelee wrinkled her nose.

"No, she just needs to know yu' OK," Lori said, rubbing her belly.

They were very close as a family, even with their mother living in London, England, for the past ten years. She had relocated to London after their father's death of a massive heart attack to live with their aunt Kay, who was also a widow. While they were in three different places, they made it a priority to visit each other, and if that wasn't possible they kept in touch by phone. She had the phone bills to prove it.

Kelee hadn't talked to her mother in two months. A sense of guilt filled her. She had always made it a priority to speak with her mother every two weeks. Two weeks turned into months; she owed her mother a call with a big apology.

As an interior decorator and stylist Kelee was well known in New York for her impeccable sense of style. Her flair for mixing modern with a touch of the classic had sealed her reputation and placed her in high demand. Her present clientele consisted of celebrities and some of New York City's elite. She had a lucrative growing business that was starting to demand that she hire permanent help. She had a guy named Ian who worked with her part-time. Ian had a remarkable eye and they worked well together. It was time she made him full-time. It would allow her to take on more clients and get some much-needed time for herself. Kelee had been working nonstop for the past two years and hadn't had time for a vacation or family. She didn't want to miss the birth of her niece and had decided to take the time off.

Taking a break from unpacking, Kelee called her mother. She answered on the second ring.

"Mama." Kelee smiled into the phone, loving the sound of her mother's voice.

"Kelee," her mother said, excited.

"I'm sorry I didn't call, I was so busy getting ready to come here," Kelee told her mother, as she clutched the phone to her ear. She moved to the window and opened it. The cool evening breeze fluttered through the curtains bringing in the scent of the hibiscus flowers beneath her windows. Kelee took a deep breath, appreciating the fresh, fragrant scent.

"So, how long yu' stayin' in St. Pala?" her mother asked.

"Until yu' grandchild is born."

"I wish I could be there." She could hear the regret in her mother's tone. Kelee knew how excited her mother was about being a grandmother and not being here was hard for her. Her mother's doctor had warned her about traveling for a while after she had broken her hip a few months ago.

"So yu' spendin' Christmas in New York, *alone, again*?" her mother asked. Kelee had spent last Christmas working. She had made plans to go to England but had to scrap them. Her client at the time needed his apartment redone for his annual New Year's Eve party. Kelee had completed the job on time, but was unable to join her mother in England for the holidays.

"I haven't made any plans for the holidays yet," Kelee told her.

"I'm comin' to St. Pala for Christmas; come see me?" She could hear the plea in her mother's voice. Once again guilt consumed her.

"I'll try." Kelee collapsed into the armchair by her bed.

"I want to see yu'," her mother demanded.

"I want to see yu', too. I'll try my best to come back," Kelee promised.

"OK." Her mother sounded pleased. "So how yu' boyfriend doin'? What's his name again?"

"We broke up." Kelee frowned. She had put so much faith into her last relationship and it had ended badly.

"Why? He was so nice."

"He was too nice, to other women."

"Dog!" her mother came out with, which made Kelee grin.

"Yu' got that right."

Her ex, Jon, was African/Italian American, and very handsome. He was an investment banker on Wall Street and a woman's dream. Kelee had walked in on him spreading his charm to his next-door neighbor. She had calmly taken whatever things she had at his place and walked out. When he had called apologizing, she told him never to call her again.

"Don't yu' worry. Yu'll find a nice man one day," her mother comforted her.

"I'm not looking. I've decided to give men a break for a while."

"Good for yu'," her mother said.

Kelee was grateful for her mother's support, which was the one thing she knew she could always rely on no matter what the situation. They spent the next half hour catching up.

Chapter 2

"Wha' yu' think?" Lori asked as she stepped from the dressing room, modeling an elegant maternity evening dress in peach chiffon. They were in a boutique on Main Street uptown, St. Pala. Kelee looked at her sister and nodded with approval; it was the perfect dress for her. They had been shopping for a dress for the past three days and Kelee was getting tired. They had an important political fund-raiser to go to tomorrow night, and they had to find something for Lori today. Unfortunately, there wasn't much to choose from on the island where high fashion was concerned. The dress her sister had on was overpriced, but that was the way it was in the Caribbean. Anything designer and imported was overpriced. Now if they were in New York, Kelee knew they would have gotten the same dress for half the price and it wouldn't have taken them this long to find one.

She did like the dress Lori had on. It accentuated her belly, yet still managed to flatter her figure. This was definitely the one. They would look no more.

"This is definitely the one," Kelee said, as she inspected the dress closer. The dress was off the shoulders and fell in layers to floor. It was absolutely perfect. They were not leaving the store without it.

"It's so hard to shop for events when yu' pregnant," Lori commented, checking her figure in the mirror with a frown.

"No more looking; this is the one," Kelee told her. This was the sixth dress Lori had tried on since they had been in the store. They had been to three other shops since morning and found nothing, until now. This dress would definitely do.

"I like it," Lori agreed.

"Good. Let's pay for this and get some lunch; I'm hungry," Kelee said. Lori headed back into the dressing room to remove the dress. It was almost two P.M., way past lunchtime, and her stomach had been protesting for the last hour.

Kelee took the dress and went to pay for it while Lori got back into her own clothes. Minutes later they left the shop in search of food. They were uptown so there was an array of exotic trendy and local restaurants to choose from.

"What's good and close by?" Kelee asked. They were standing on a busy sidewalk just outside the store. The hot afternoon sun beat down on them. Kelee wiped away the sweat forming on her upper lip as she slipped on her shades.

"Tali's. It's just down the next street." Lori led the way.

"This is good," Kelee said as she enjoyed her fresh lobster pasta salad. Kelee paused and smiled at Lori, who was busy with her curry-coconut shrimp and rice. They were seated in the patio area of the restaurant. It was bustling with a late afternoon crowd of regulars and tourists. St. Pala, like most islands in the Caribbean, had an eclectic mix of cultures. It was an island rich in minerals, sugar, and coffee. The economy was growing steadily with new businesses. Most of the east and west ends of St. Pala catered towards tourists offering some of the most exquisite resorts in the Caribbean. Downtown St. Pala City was the financial center of the island, with its bustling businesses. Downtown was the heart of St. Pala. It offered the best of everything. Kelee loved to shop here because it offered the best bargains on the island.

As Kelee watched her sister eat, she smiled, knowing she was eating for two. Lori gazed up at her and smiled, sipping her fruit punch. While they waited for dessert, Kelee went to the bathroom. When she made her way back to the table, she saw him. From his profile, she could tell he was fine. He kissed Lori's cheek, smiling down at her. The first thing Kelee noticed about him was his muscular physique; he wasn't big or bulky, he was just right. His polo shirt clung to his incredible biceps. Nice, very nice. She smiled.

"How yu' doin'?" the man asked, touching Lori's belly. Kelee noted his deep, rich Caribbean accent, definitely a native. He definitely worked out, she could tell by his muscle tone. She wondered what he looked like naked. She paused in her steps. She didn't even know the man and here she was lusting after him. For all she knew he was probably married with kids. She looked at his hand; no wedding band. That still didn't mean anything. A lot of married men didn't wear their wedding rings.

"Good. Good to have yu' back." Lori smiled up at the man. Kelee's eyes traveled down the rest of his body: nice ass and nice thighs. Damn, he was fine. As if sensing her, the man looked up and paused. His face was borderline perfect with a square jaw and a slightly straight nose. He had smooth caramel-colored skin, his hair black and wavy. His lush lips were inviting. Kelee reached the table; she kept her gaze locked on him. The man continued to stare at her from behind his shades. Kelee wished she could see his eyes.

He straightened up to his full height. He was almost six feet and he smelled good. He continued to stare at her. She wondered if he was as intrigued as she was. After all, he was staring, which was a good thing.

"Sean, this is my sister Kelee. Kelee, Sean St. John," Lori introduced them with a wide grin on her face.

"Nice to meet yu', Sean." Kelee smiled and extended her hand to him.

Sean took her hand as he took off his shades. Slanted hazel eyes met hers. Suddenly Kelee had a feeling that she knew him, but from where? She had seen those eyes before, but where? She couldn't place them.

"Kelee." The way he said her name with such familiarity sent thrills down her spine. Kelee searched her brain trying to figure out where she knew him from, but nothing clicked. Why was he so familiar?

"Sean, join us?" Lori suggested.

"Can't, I have a meetin'." He glanced at Lori.

"Yu' must come by for dinner so we can catch up," Lori insisted.

"I'd like that," he said and looked at Kelee with such knowing intensity that it made her even more curious. If he didn't know her, then he obviously knew of her. "Kelee." He nodded to her, then hurried off. Kelee watched him disappear into the restaurant.

"So who is he?" she asked casually as she sat down. Lori smiled, digging into her pineapple upside-down cake.

"Fine, isn't he?"

"Excuse me, married lady." Kelee glared at her, amused.

"I'm married, not blind; plus, I was referrin' to yu'."

"Who said I was interested?" Kelee responded.

"Yu' eyes did."

Kelee was a bit embarrassed. Had she really stared at him that badly? "Leave my eyes out of this."

"Don't worry, yu'll see him again at the party tomorrow night." Lori grinned.

Kelee had to admit that the idea of seeing Sean St. John again excited her. There was something about him.

"Yu' still haven't told me who he is."

"He's our minister of security."

"He's a cop?" Kelee couldn't help but be disappointed on hearing he was a cop. She frowned and shrugged.

"He's more than a cop, he protects the entire island," Lori added.

While Kelee didn't care for cops, she couldn't help but wondering about Sean St. John.

"What's his mix?" His slanted hazel eyes had her curious.

"His mother is Chinese and his father is West Indian. He's single and much sought after." Lori bounced her brows at her.

Kelee got the hint. "I'm sure he is." Kelee grinned. "As fine as he is."

Lori laughed, finishing off her cake.

* * *

Sean St. John barely paid any attention to what Carl Wess had said during their business lunch. Kelee Kingsly was all he could think about. She was back in St. Pala. He had prayed for this day for the past ten years; now it was here. What he didn't expect was her not recognizing him. Another surprising fact was that she was Lori's sister. He had known Lori for years, had always heard her talk about her sister in New York, but he had never thought they would be the same person. He knew at least four different Kelees, so the name wasn't foreign to him. He never thought to put them together.

Sean had met Kelee on the beach while he was staying on the west coast at his father's beach cottage. When they had first met he was going through his Rasta phase, with long dreads and a full beard. Granted, he looked a lot different then, but how could she not recognize him? The memory of their five-night love affair was still fresh in his mind. She was the first woman he had fallen in love with, the only woman he had ever loved.

Kelee was seventeen when they met. The attraction was immediate and electric; the intensity of their passion was still fresh in his mind. The nights they had spent together exploring each other bought back pleasurable memories. He was twenty-one at the time and thought she was at least nineteen, until she told him her age after they had made love and he had discovered that she was a virgin. The way she had come on to him, he would have never thought she was untouched. She knew what she wanted and he was more than willing to give it to her. She had wrapped him around her little finger with her incredible budding body. She still had that incredible body, only more matured. She had filled out nicely; he recalled her now fuller breasts and rounded hips. She was cute then, now she was stunningly beautiful. After five nights at his beach house totally enthralled in each other, she had disappeared. No good-byes, nothing. Now she was back and she had no idea who he was. The thought of it made him laugh.

Sean headed downtown to his office. As usual, the streets were swamped with traffic and vendors, taking him an extra ten minutes before he reached the municipal building parking lot. The municipal building reflected its colonial heritage with its stippled roof and slated windows. The municipal building housed a number of government offices. His office, which was the Office of Defense, was housed on the first floor of the building. He made his way down the old marble corridor to his office. His receptionist Clair was gone for the day. He tapped on his partner Jack Henry's half-open door to let him know he was in the office.

In his office, Sean unholstered his gun, which he wore behind his back, then dropped into his plush chair. His office was large, with a view of the back parking lot. The walls were lined with file cabinets and in one corner sat a shelf of surveillance equipment. He was about to make a call when Jack walked in, tapping on his door.

"Wha' yu' have on Mike?" Sean asked Jack Henry as he sat behind his desk. Jack was his right-hand man, and a damn good undercover special agent. Jack was a tall, thick, dark-skinned man with haunting, cold green eyes. His eyes gave him an intimidating look, which worked well in their line of work.

"The boat was clean." Jack frowned. His heavy voice boomed off the walls. Sean shared in Jack's disappointment; they had been watching Mike Curve for the past year. Curve was a businessman and a ruthless killer who used his business and his connections to traffic drugs on and off the island. Curve was a hard man to touch, mainly because he remained so visible, and of course there were his connections on and off St. Pala. Getting to Curve was proving to be more and more difficult as the days went by. Not being able to catch him was starting to frustrate the hell out of Sean. Curve knew he was after him, and was good at eluding him. But Sean was determined to bring him down no matter what it took. Drugs were starting to destroy his island and he would do anything to stop it. One way or the other he intended to get rid of Curve.

Sean's most recent victory over Curve was taking down three of his men in a drug bust off the north coast. That was three months ago. Drugs were still leaking into St. Pala, and his job was to put a stop to it. Not being able to get to Curve was starting to frustrate Sean; he needed something tangible on him and he needed it soon! But Curve had too many people in his pocket, which made it damn near impossible to get to him. To make matters worse, Curve's legitimate businesses on the island provided cover for him. But Sean knew he would slip up one day, and he would be there to get him.

"So we have no'ting," Sean said, frustrated.

"He has too many eyes."

"We need to put out his eyes." Sean knew he had to get working on Mike's informers or he'd get nowhere fast.

His thoughts drifted to Kelee, and he smiled. Kelee was a whole different matter, a pleasurable one. Her return to St. Pala was at a bad time, but he would make do with the time he had to deal with her.

"Wha'?" Jack asked, snapping Sean back to reality.

"Wha'?"

"Who is she?"

"Who?"

"The woman yu' was thinkin' of?" Jack gave him a knowing look. They had known each other all their lives and were close friends; actually they were more like brothers. They could read each other like a book, which worked well with their partner- friendship.

"Someone from my past."

"She must be som'ting." A slow grin curled Jack's lips.

"She is," he admitted, smiling. The way she had looked at him told him she found him attractive. He couldn't wait to get his hands on her.

"If she have yu' smilin' like that, I can't wait to meet her," Jack said, intrigued.

Sean suddenly remembered an invitation he had gotten about a fund-raiser tomorrow night. Lori and Allan would be there and so would Kelee.

"Call me on the mobile if yu' need me. I have to pick up a suit for tomorrow night." Sean jumped out of his chair and headed for the door.

"I thought yu' weren't goin'."

"Change of plans . . ." He paused with a silly grin on his face.

"She's goin' to be there? I wonder if Mavis up for a party tomorrow night?" Jack laughed. Mavis was Jack's wife of ten years. They had gotten married right out of high school and had four kids, whom Sean was godfather to.

Sean simply smiled and ran out the door. He could hear Jack's laughter booming behind him. He hadn't planned on attending the fund-raiser but now her being there was incentive enough for him to go to the fund-raiser.

* * *

It was almost six P.M. and most of the businesses and shops were already closed for the day, except for the restaurants and a few small shops and supermarkets. Sean raced uptown with his siren blasting, making it to his favorite men's shop just in time before they closed their doors. The manager knew him and let him in immediately. He told the sales lady exactly what he wanted and she found his size and style in a few minutes. Sean checked in with Jack before he headed home. His house was a located on a hill, overlooking the city. It was farther up the hill than most homes, which he loved. Driving through his security gates he drove down a short path to his house. His home was a two-level luxury house, painted cream and pale blue. His father had built it ten years ago. It had six bedrooms, a living room, a dining room and an eat-in kitchen with a separate dining area. He had put in a pool and a Jacuzzi a couple of years ago. The main attraction of the house was the veranda. It surrounded the entire house, offering a spectacular view of the city below and the mountains as a backdrop. The servant's apartment was just off the garage, where his housekeeper May lived. The house was far too big for him, of course, and his mother kept pestering him about filling it with a wife and children. Sean knew he would marry one day, but the right woman was key to all that. He thought of Kelee; she was definitely wife material. Any man would love to have her on his arm. She was spirited and fun when they had first met; he wondered if she was still the same.

Sean parked his jeep in the garage and got out, taking his suit with him. He walked to the end of the driveway and looked down at the house with the red slate roof. Kelee was under that roof and the knowledge of her being so close excited him. Sean wasn't a man who got excited over a woman often. They threw themselves at him. He had plenty to choose from. But seeing Kelee again had confirmed it: he hadn't gotten over her. How the hell didn't she recognize him? He stood there staring at the house. A wicked smile touched his lips. He wondered how she'd react when she found out who he really was. He couldn't wait to find out, but for now he would simply play along.

Sean headed inside, the scent of freshly cut flowers in the foyer welcoming him. At first, he had reservations about moving in after his parents moved to Florida. They wanted to be near their five grandchildren. Sean had lived at home since he was nineteen when he joined the intelligence force. He made his way into the kitchen to find May humming and washing dishes. May Brown was an older woman, in her late fifties. She had been working for him for the past five years. She was very motherly to him, which he didn't mind with his own mother now living in Florida. May was a widow and her children were living in Brooklyn, New York. She only visited them once a year, because of her fear of flying. She was short and round with salt and pepper hair, which she wore in braids under her headscarf. Her skin was leathery and brown from being in the sun too much. May had worked on a cocoa plantation most of her life and it showed in her sun-wrinkled skin.

"Yu' dinner is ready," May told him and pointed to the plate covered by a red mesh dome on the counter. He moved over to the plate and lifted the cover. She had made him his favorite—yellow yam and steamed snapper with okra. His mouth watered at the scent of the food. He placed it in the microwave for two minutes. He had barely eaten lunch, distracted from seeing Kelee earlier.

"Yu' OK?" May asked. He looked up at her and swallowed. "Yu' kinda quiet. Some'ting wrong?" May was good at picking up when something wasn't right with him or he wasn't himself.

"No, no, every'ting fine." He grinned.

May gave him a scrutinizing look before going back to the dishes. Sean went back to his food, thinking of Kelee. He couldn't wait for tomorrow night. It still tickled him that she didn't remember him.

Chapter 3

Kelee couldn't stop thinking of Sean St. John. She was excited over the fact that he might be at the party tonight. All day she had dreamed of seeing him again. She didn't know what it was about him that had her so interested. Maybe it was his eyes—they were so familiar to her. She had gone to bed thinking of him and woke up thinking of him. It was crazy, but she couldn't wait to see him again. She couldn't even remember the last time a man had captured her attention from such a brief meeting.

The dress Kelee had decided to wear to the fund-raiser was a sexy strapless peach number made of chiffon. The dress had an empire waist that hugged and lifted her breasts before falling into an A-line skirt to her ankles. She chose high-heeled black sling-back pumps with a matching black clutch. Around her neck she wore a single string of amber and in her ears she wore the matching stud earrings. She had pinned her hair back behind her ears with crystal clips. She checked herself one last time in the mirror before leaving her room.

Allan and Lori were ready and waiting in the sitting room. Allan was massaging Lori's belly, his favorite thing to do, she had noticed since arriving. He was connected to his unborn child, which was a beautiful thing. They made a beautiful couple.

"Lookin' good," Allan commented, looking her over with admiration.

"Thank yu'." She smiled at the six-foot giant of a man. Allan was West Indian/white with black hair, bronze coloring, and blue eyes. Kelee wondered whom her niece would take after.

They got into Allan's BMW and headed down the hill, then crosstown to Jove Hall—a grand house used mainly for entertaining and a tourist attraction. It was the first main governor's house built on the island. It was a grand sight surrounded by endless gardens and lawns. It was also the most popular spot for wedding receptions. The grounds and the fountain were well lit, welcoming its guests. The hall was buzzing with well dressed dignitaries, politicians, and the elite of St. Pala.

Champagne was ever flowing with some delectable Caribbean infused hors d'oeuvres. Kelee got herself a glass of champagne, while Allan went to the bar to get Lori some juice. Kelee scanned the room but she didn't see Sean.

"Yu' think Sean will be here?" Kelee looked at Lori. Lori gave her a mischievous look before responding. "He's not one for parties."

"Oh." Kelee sipped her drink, disappointed. She had hoped to see him tonight.

Allan returned with juice for Lori. He had barely handed her her drink, when some of his friends whisked him off.

"How do yu' even find quality time with him?" Kelee asked.

"Trust me, we do, or I wouldn't be in this state." Lori grinned and rubbed her stomach. Kelee touched her sister's stomach and smiled. Lori was extremely patient. She knew what it was like being a politician's wife and she handled it all so well. Kelee commended her for her patience.

"Hello, ladies," a deep voice said behind them. Kelee instantly recognized Sean's voice and excitement raced through her. She turned to look at him. The sight of him was a pleasure. Kelee allowed a gentle smile to reach her lips. She had to keep her excitement in check; she didn't want him to see the effect he had on her. He was striking in a gray suit that hung just right on his muscular frame. Damn, he was fine!

His eyes met and held hers as he dropped a kiss on Lori's cheek. His eyes were so familiar to her. Anxiety coupled with curiosity filled her stomach, making it quiver. She got the feeling of knowing him, which was strange, seeing that she didn't know him. She was looking forward to knowing him, if he was available.

He smiled at Kelee and his face came alive with his million-dollar smile. His teeth were even and perfect—and those lips! She blinked and rescued her thoughts from just how much she wanted Sean St. John. She hadn't felt this kind of attraction since she was a teenager. He moved to sit beside her and she caught the scent of his cologne. His cool scent invaded her senses, stimulating her in ways that surprised her. *Stay cool.* She really had to get some control. Maybe her stay in St. Pala wasn't going to be so boring. She smiled inwardly, looking into his handsome face. Not that being here for her niece's birth was boring. All she knew was that Sean was definitely the kind of man she would love to occupy her free time with.

"Thought yu' didn't do social events?" Lori gave Sean a questioning look.

"This one is different," he commented, never taking his eyes off Kelee. She blushed under his piercing eyes. "Kelee," he greeted her with that infectious smile of his.

"Nice to see yu' again," she said coolly.

"Yu' too," he said. "Can I borrow Kelee for a second?" he asked Lori, but kept his eyes solely fixed on her.

"Sure, my husband looks like he needs rescuin'." Lori looked at Allan. Sean assisted her out of her chair. Lori thanked him and headed towards Allan. He held a hand out to her. Kelee placed her hand in his strong warm hand. He gently helped her up, placing a hand around her waist, and led her from the hall. He grabbed fresh drinks before leading her out into the gardens.

"Is this yu' first time in St. Pala?" He directed her towards a bench. He sat beside her.

"No, it's my third trip." She took a sip of her drink, loving how the light of the garden made his hair shine.

"And we've never met until now?" he asked, intrigued.

Kelee smirked. "Guess not."

"How long yu' stayin'?" His eyes held hers with such intensity, she felt like baring her soul to him. That was not good; she didn't even know the man.

"Until Lori has her baby."

"Then yu' go back to New York?" He sounded disappointed. She studied him and he seemed genuinely disappointed.

"Yes." She looked at him, curious. "How did yu' know I was from New York?"

"Lori."

Kelee couldn't help but grin. "So yu' know about me?"

"Not enough." His eyes searched hers with such earnestness, she had to take a breath and focus her thoughts. "I want to know more," he continued.

"Like what?" She smiled, enjoying his inquiry.

"Wha' exactly yu' do in New York."

"I'm a decorator and stylist. Lori told me that yu' the minister of security. Do yu' like what yu' do?" She came back with a question of her own.

"I used to be an undercover cop, so it was an easy transition," he told her with a confident ease.

"So yu' like what yu' do?"

"I wouldn't do it if I didn't; an' yu'?"

She smiled. "I love what I do. I get to meet new and interesting people." She loved her career mainly because of the different people she interacted with on a daily basis.

"So can I see yu' while yu' here?" Kelee was a little thrown by his bold request. The man wasted no time, not that she minded.

"I don't know." She eyed him with caution.

"Yu' don't know?" He raised a surprised brow at her.

"I just met yu'."

"Then have lunch with me tomorrow, so yu' can get to know me." He smiled and she knew she couldn't say no.

"Yu' waste no time, do yu'?"

"Why should I, when I know wha' I want?" he said with such sexy confidence, it excited and intrigued her at the same time; Kelee had forgotten how bold Caribbean men could be; especially when it came to a woman they wanted.

"And what exactly do yu' want?" She had to challenge him.

A sensuous smile crossed his lips and his eyes darkened with desire. "The same 'ting yu' want."

Kelee's mind went wild with that possibility. There was a lot she wanted from him, starting with his body. She hadn't had sex in months and he was an intoxicating man. Kelee couldn't help the smile that touched her lips. He knew she was attracted to him and he wasn't about to play coy.

"What about yu' woman?"

"Don't have one," he responded smoothly. She glared at him in disbelief. No man as fine as he was would be without a woman. St. Pala was known for its beautiful women, so she didn't buy the fact that he wasn't attached.

"Yu' mean not at the moment, right?" She studied him to see if he'd lie. He laughed, flashing perfect white teeth. Kelee had grown up in Jamaica, against experts when it came to sweet-talking a woman into believing anything. She was sure Sean St. John wasn't any different. Men like him would say and do anything to get a woman they wanted. Yes, she wanted him, too, but she had to know what he was about first. He was the sexy, confident, strong type, which she found extremely attractive. She wondered about his flaws; he had to have a few.

"Wha' 'bout yu'?" Sean looked her over with

renewed interest. The heat from his eyes made her tingle.

"Single," she said and watched as his eyes gleamed with approval.

"Good; so we shouldn't have a problem."

"I guess not." She smiled at him and finished her drink. They heard the sound of a microphone check.

"The ceremony is startin'," Sean said and offered her a hand, which he gently gripped as he pulled her to her feet. He dropped a hand around her waist and pulled her close to him, smiling down at her. Her body reacted to his closeness by sending tingles rippling beneath her skin. The cool scent of his cologne was soothing. She leaned against him as he led her inside, but she didn't want to go back inside, she wanted to stay where they were and get to know him better. He kept her close to his side as he guided her to where Lori was seated. He helped her into her chair and pulled his right up next to hers. Kelee smiled, enjoying the attention. Lori looked at them, grinning.

Kelee barely heard what the speakers said, all because Sean was by her side. He draped his arm across the back of her chair. As the speakers changed, Sean would whisper to her who they were. The warmth of his breath against her ear and neck was seriously starting to turn her on. A break came and Sean went to get them drinks. Allan rejoined them. He pulled his chair closer to Lori, caressing her belly. Lori gazed at him lovingly.

Sean returned with her drink. She smiled at him, thanking him.

"Thought yu' didn't do parties?" Allan said, shaking Sean's hand.

Sean simply gazed at Kelee. His look said it all; he was definitely here because of her. Kelee blushed and took a sip of her drink.

"I see." Allan chuckled.

"I couldn't pass up such an . . ." Sean started to speak, but stopped suddenly. Kelee gazed at him to see a cold hard look on his face. His eyes were focused across the room. The coldness in his eyes was a bit jarring.

"Wha' the hell is he doin' here?" Sean's harsh tone sent alarming chills down Kelee's spine.

Allan looked in the direction that Sean was referring to. Kelee followed his gaze. The man they were focused on was a tall, strikingly handsome man. The man stared back at them with a conceited smirk. Kelee looked at Sean and saw intense hate in his eyes. She couldn't help wondering what the man had done to him to garner such hate. Kelee looked back at the man to find him staring at her with alarming interest. The man's gaze set off her caution light. She looked back at Sean to find him still focused on the man. He then looked at her with regret.

"Good night," Sean announced, got up, and walked off without looking back. Kelee stared at

Sean's back, stunned. She couldn't fathom what had just happened.

"What the hell was that about?" Kelee asked, upset. What was his problem? If he was going to act like that, she wasn't sure she really wanted to know him. No matter how fine he was.

Allan shrugged but Kelee got the feeling he knew more. The look of contemplation on his face said it all. The man across the room had something to do with Sean leaving so abruptly. But what?

"Excuse me," Allan said and hurried off after Sean.

"What am I missing here?" Kelee inquired.

"Beats me," Lori said, looking just as confused.

"Hey, man, wait up," Allan called out. Sean stopped and turned to see Allan running up to him.

"Who was dat?" Allan asked, catching his breath.

"Mike's brother, Kurt," Sean said harshly.

Allan pulled back, surprised. "He's got some nerve showin' his face like that."

"They're tauntin' me."

"How yu' know that?"

"My last bust failed, someone tipped them off." Sean couldn't even disguise the frustration in his voice. He and Allan were on the same side, so he understood.

"Yu' know who?"

"No, but whoever it is, he's playin' both sides. It's the only way they could have gotten the heads-up on wha' we were doin'."

Allan looked at him, concerned. "Wha' can I do?"

"Keep yu' eyes and ears open."

"So why yu' leavin' the party?"

"Did yu' see the way he was lookin' at Kelee?"

"I understand."

"Tell her I'll call." Sean really didn't want to leave but he had to.

"No problem."

"Thanks; later." Sean walked off towards his car. He got on his cell phone, informing the coast guard to be extra vigilant tonight. He slammed his hand against the steering wheel in anger. He had lost three men in the pursuit already. He knew how ruthless Mike's people could be. He didn't want anyone close to him to be a target. He thought of Kelee. He really didn't want to leave her tonight. While his intention was to seduce her tonight, he also couldn't put her in harm's way. He didn't want her becoming a target.

Chapter 4

Kelee browsed through the rack of baby clothes. There were so many things to choose from, she didn't even know where to start. She had left Lori in the doctor's office next door, where she was getting a checkup. The nurse had told her the exam would take a while, so she decided to browse in the store while she waited.

"Nice choice," Sean's voice echoed behind her.

"Yu' think so?" she asked, turning to glare at him. She was still mad at him for disappearing the way he did last night.

"Yes," he said in his sexy confident voice as his eyes smiled down at her.

"I hope yu' not stalking me?"

He looked her over, lust lurking in his beautiful eyes. Kelee was wearing a short khaki skirt and a halter. She got warm under his open, alluring gaze. It amazed her how he could look at her with such open lust. Not that she minded. She rather liked it—coming from him, of course.

"That's a pleasant thought," he said in a sultry tone that caused her breasts to tingle. She let out a slight breath; he was good—maybe too good; this could make him dangerous.

"I shouldn't even be talking to yu', especially with the way yu' left last night." She tried to sound serious, but it was difficult with him looking at her like that.

"I know, an' I'm grateful." He sounded sincere enough.

"Care to tell me about it?"

"Security reasons," he responded calmly.

"And?" She wanted a better answer.

"Join me for lunch?"

So she wasn't going to get an answer to her question. "Sorry, I'm waiting for Lori," she threw at him coldly.

"The restaurant is just across the street, we can talk there," he pleaded. "We can leave a message for Lori to join us when she's done with her checkup."

Kelee looked at him, surprised. "How did yu' know she was gettin' a checkup?"

"My cousin is her doctor." He smiled.

She looked into his very familiar, smiling eyes, and got that feeling of knowing him again.

"I don't think I want to have lunch with yu'," she said, unable to hide her smile.

"With that smile I beg to differ," he said with a confident smirk. He gently touched her cheek, looking her deeply in the eyes, and said, "Please?"

"I guess I could shop later," Kelee gave in. She was mad at him for leaving the way he did at the party, but she also couldn't deny the fact that she was happy to see him.

"Good." He took her hand, leading her from the store.

Moments later they were seated in the cool bright interior of the Chinese/Caribbean restaurant, which was almost packed with the noon crowd. A beautiful mocha-skinned waitress took their order. Kelee ordered the coconut shrimp over lo mein. Sean ordered the seafood combination served over white rice. Bob Marley music played in the background, creating a mellow mood.

"What exactly do yu' do?" Kelee asked, taking a sip of her fresh pineapple juice.

"The core of my work goes into keepin' drugs from gettin' on and off de' island."

"Sounds dangerous."

"It can be," he admitted.

"And yu' like risking yu' life like that?"

"I have to protect the welfare of my people." He studied her. "Yu' don't approve?"

"Someone has to protect the island, right?" She shrugged. She was starting to like him, but the idea of him being a cop weighed heavily on her.

"Yu' don't like cops?" he asked.

Memories of her ex-boyfriend, who was a New York City cop, pulling his gun on her when he thought she was cheating flashed before her eyes. If it hadn't been for her roommate knocking him unconscious he probably would have shot her. He was arrested for reckless endangerment and kicked off the force. When he had found out she hadn't been cheating on him, he had tried his best to win her back. That night would remain with her forever.

"Wha' is it?" Sean asked, touching her hand. Kelee jumped. He looked at her, concerned. "Yu' OK?"

"Yeah, I'm fine." She pushed her memories aside. It was behind her, yet the horror of what had almost happened to her was still with her.

"Wha' did he do to yu'?" Sean asked.

"What?" Kelee was surprised he had read her so accurately.

"The cop who put that fear in yu' eyes?" Sean's eyes searched hers.

"How could yu' tell that?"

"The way yu' reacted just now."

Kelee looked into Sean's familiar eyes. What was it about him that pulled at her so? She got lost in his eyes, wondering if she could trust him. His eyes told her she could. Her heart told her to be careful.

"He thought I was cheating on him. He probably would have killed me if my roommate hadn't knocked him out."

"Jesus."

"That's why I don't care for cops," she told him.

"I guess I don't look too good to yu' right now?" Sean gave her a reassuring smile.

"I really try not to be too judgmental, but yu' can understand my hesitation, can't yu'?"

"I do, but I 'tink there's som'ting between us that's worth explorin', don't yu'?" He smiled.

"Have yu' ever pulled yu' gun on a woman?" Kelee watched as his smile vanished.

"Not one that I've dated."

Kelee looked at him wanting to believe him. A part of her remained skeptical.

"I've never even raised my hand at a woman," he continued. "I've seen too many battered women in my line of work. No way in hell I'd add to that."

Kelee believed him; she didn't know why, but she did. She relaxed and enjoyed the rest of her lunch with him. Lori joined them just as they were about to order dessert. She dropped into the chair, breathing hard.

"I'm so hungry." She reached for a breadstick.

The waitress came over and handed Lori a menu. Kelee and Sean watched amused as Lori order the largest serving of shrimp lo mein on the menu with egg rolls and fruit punch.

"Wha' yu' two smilin' at? I'm eatin' for two now."

"That's just an excuse," Sean teased. Kelee nodded in agreement. Lori rolled her eyes at them.

"Hush up!" Lori demanded, hiding a smile.

A low beep went off and Sean reached for his phone on his hip.

"Excuse me, ladies," he told them before he answered his phone. "Speak . . ." he said into his phone. Suddenly his face took on a serious expression. "Give me ten minutes," he said and switched off his phone. "I have to go." Kelee looked at him, disappointed. He was running off again. He smiled and winked at her; it caused Kelee to smile despite her disappointment.

"I'm cookin' tomorrow an' I want yu' over for dinner at five," Lori told Sean as he stood up to leave.

"Make it six an' I'll be there." Sean dropped a kiss on Lori's cheek. "I got the bill." He smiled at Kelee. "See yu' tomorrow." He squeezed her hand before leaving.

"How was the checkup?" Kelee asked Lori after watching Sean leave.

"Probing. I see yu' two gettin' along."

"How long have yu' known him?"

"About eight years," Lori responded.

"How come I didn't meet him the last time I was here?"

"I think he was trainin' in the States then," Lori said. The waitress brought her the egg rolls and sauce. Lori thanked her and bit into an egg roll.

"So yu' like him?" Lori asked with her mouth full.

"He's OK." Kelee shrugged.

"But he's a cop, right?" Lori swallowed and looked at her for an answer. "Sean's one of the few decent ones out there."

"Does he have any kids?"

"Why?"

"I just want to know."

"No; none that I know of," Lori added, starting on another egg roll. Kelee smiled at her sister as she watched her attack her food.

"Slow down, yu' might choke," Kelee warned.

"Tell that to this baby," Lori mumbled, finishing off another egg roll.

Sean drove like a madman to the location Jack had given him. His heart raced with anxiety over his missing men. He whipped past overloaded mini-buses, cars, and bikes on the expressway, his siren blasting. Ten minutes later he turned off the main road and down a narrow stone path with thorn shrubs on both sides. He came to the end of the road where a small dilapidated shack sat just off the old dock. It was an isolated area where a small boat could dock. Sean saw Jack's Land Rover as he pulled up. Jack got out of his jeep as he approached.

"Any'ting yet?" he asked.

"No'ting."

"Ra'ass," Sean cursed. He had two of his best investigators, Adams and Penn, stationed out here. They hadn't heard from them in four hours. There wasn't any vehicle in sight, which worried him. Something wasn't right; he could feel it resonating in his bones. He couldn't afford to lose another man. "OK, take the back, I got the front. Be careful."

Jack nodded with a knowing grin. Sean knew Jack. He would shoot first and ask questions later. Simultaneously they pulled their guns and approached the shack with caution. Sean approached the front door with care. He knew there was only one window and it was in the back. Jack had that covered. Sean stepped carefully, taking care not to make any noise. He carefully tried the doorknob. It was locked. He stepped back, took a breath, and kicked the door in. Quickly he stepped aside in case whoever was inside started firing. Nothing. He listened for a few minutes; nothing. He entered with caution, gun ready. The smell of urine and stale liquor hit him like a rock. Quickly he scanned the room. It was empty. He was relieved but concerned. Where were his men?

"Clear," he called out. Moments later Jack joined him inside the shack. They looked around the room for any evidence. All that was in the room was a dirty mattress and a three-legged chair turned over in the corner.

"If no one's here, why was the door locked?" Sean scanned the room more closely. He saw nothing.

"Some'ting not right. Where the hell are Adams an' Penn?" Jack said, worried.

"Try the mobile?" Sean said, holstering his gun. Jack pulled out his phone and dialed. A few seconds later, they heard a muffled ring. Instantly they looked to the mattress. The muffled ring came again from under the mattress. Sean approached it and flipped it, in one quick move. The phone was on the floor, ringing. Sean and Jack looked at each other, worried. They both knew this was not good. Jack ended the call.

"Let's do a two-mile search before I call in the search party," Sean said. Jack nodded in agreement. They searched the area surrounding the cabin, and came up with nothing.

Back to the office, Sean called in a search party to comb the area and the waters off the docks.

"I should have known he was up to some'ting when I saw Hal at the party last night," Sean said, contemplating the safety of his men.

"He's gettin' bolder every day," Jack said and handed him a Guinness Stout. Sean took the cold drink and took a large gulp.

It was getting late and the search party hadn't found anything. He dreaded calling it off, but it was getting dark and he knew they wouldn't be able to find anything in the dark.

They knew that Mike and Hal were ruthless killers. Sean's biggest fear at the moment was that his men were dead. But he had to have faith that they were still alive. He prayed they would be, for their families' sake.

"Want me to call the families?" Jack asked. Sean didn't want them worried over nothing when he had no evidence.

"No, not yet."

Jack looked at him, concerned. "Wha' next?"

"We need to find his informant," Sean said.

"I know someone who might be able to help. But he's not cheap."

"How much we talkin'?"

"Let me look into it."

"Do it." Sean rubbed his temples; he felt a headache coming on. He needed to sleep.

Chapter 5

Kelee had just dropped Lori off at a luncheon for a committee meeting. Knowing it would be another two hours before the meeting ended, she decided to browse the stalls of the crafts market a few blocks away. It was about one P.M. in the afternoon and the sun was bright and hot. Kelee parked the car in one of the shaded empty spaces outside of the plaza. It was not pleasant to get into a car that had been sitting in the naked sun, especially on a hot day downtown.

He watched Kelee step from the car. Her shapely legs were perfect in platform cork mules. She wore a flirty short skirt and a midriff T-shirt. Her hair was in a high ponytail off her neck. A small bag was tucked under her arm. She squinted against the bright sun as she made her way towards the craft market. A sweet smile curved his lips. They were right; she was beautiful—and sexy as hell to boot. He watched the sway of her behind as she climbed the few steps to one of the entrances of the building.

Kelee paused as her eyes adjusted to the dimmer light of the building. She needed a nice painting for her bedroom and whatever else caught her eye. The minute she had entered the building a vendor insisted on her taking a look at her booth. After visiting about six booths and not finding anything she liked, Kelee started to get hungry. She had had a light breakfast this morning of coffee, toast, and fruits. She looked at her watch, noting the time. She had little over an hour before she picked up Lori.

There was a restaurant across the street; she decided to go there for lunch. At the entrance of the craft market she slipped her shades on.

Just across the parking lot a man resembling Sean made his way to his car. Kelee found herself smiling as thoughts of Sean St. John flooded her consciousness. She couldn't wait to see him again. He was all she could think of since she had met him. Her stomach protested loudly, pulling her from her steamy thoughts of Sean. She looked at the restaurant across the street and contemplated whether she should drive over to their parking lot, or just walk over. Suddenly she was shoved hard from behind; she had to grab on to a pole. Her bag was ripped from her shoulders, and a man ran past her.

"Hey! Thief!" she screamed. "Thief!" she screamed even louder a second time. A number of people came running out of the market building. Kelee watched as the man dodged traffic across the street, then disappeared between two buildings. She swore as she watched one of her favorite bags disappear. Her money was gone. Kelee stood there at a loss.

"Yu' OK?" a deep male voice asked behind her and Kelee turned to find a man of rich brown complexion looking at her in concern. Dark penetrating eyes held hers. Kelee looked at him, taking in his expensive linen attire. He was over six feet and well built. His height made him a bit intimidating. Kelee took a step back.

"Are yu' OK?" he asked again.

Kelee focused. "Yes, I'm fine, but my bag is gone." Just then Kelee remembered that the car keys were in the bag. She swore. "The car keys are in my bag." Kelee headed towards where the car was parked. She gasped in shock when she saw that the car was gone. She let out a string of curses. Her bag was gone, now the car. Had she really stood out that much that someone had targeted her? Her stomach growled in hunger even louder. She really needed that money. She would have to interrupt Lori's meeting. She dreaded telling Lori about losing her new Lexus. Allan had just bought Lori the car for her birthday a few months ago. Damn it!

"Is there someone yu' can call?" the man asked, holding out his cell phone to her. Kelee looked at him. That was nice of him. "When yu' shop downtown it's a bit more risky than being uptown," the man informed her.

"Do I stand out that much?" she asked. As she finished her sentence she realized how silly she sounded. While she was comfortable in St. Pala, she was still a foreigner and foreigners were targets, especially downtown.

The man looked her over and smiled. "Yu' stunnin' and very stylish."

Kelee couldn't help but smile at his compliment, but this was not the time or the place for compliments: her bag and her sister's car were stolen. She kicked herself for not being as careful as she should have been. She should have known better; she was downtown, not uptown. She turned to stare at the spot where she had parked the car and contemplated her next move. She needed to get back to Lori. Kelee really didn't want to interrupt her, but Lori had to know her car was stolen. The police also had to be informed. This was a mess. She had never been robbed before, not even in New York City. She felt stripped; she didn't like it at all.

Lori was three long blocks away and the sun was piping hot. Kelee didn't know if she could make it there without passing out. She looked down the long, hot, bare road and bit her lips.

"I can't believe this is happening to me," she moaned in frustration.

"Tell yu' wha'. I was just 'bout to have lunch across the street. Let's get out of the sun. Yu' can make yu' call from there and get some'ting to drink."

"I was about to go there to eat when that ass stole my bag."

"So join me for a drink? Yu' look like yu' could use one."

Kelee knew he was right. She was thirsty, hungry, and sweating. However, she had to be careful: she didn't know him.

"Thanks, but no."

"Yu' can't just stand here," he pointed out.

She knew he was right. At the moment she could use the help, but her guard was up—especially after what had just happened.

"Thanks, but I don't know yu'," she responded.

"Tyce." He held a hand out to her with the most infectious smile. She looked at his hand before taking it.

"Kelee," she said.

He shook her hand gently. "Kelee, that's pretty." His smile was comforting.

"Thanks," she said.

"Care to join me?" He gestured towards the

restaurant. What harm was in it anyway? Her throat was parched; she could use a cool drink.

"Only for a drink, then I have to call my sister."

"OK," he said and led her through the parking lot, across the street, and into the cool restaurant. The restaurant was called Yams. Its billboard outside advertised traditional dishes.

"Welcome, Mr. T." The hostess greeted them with a bright smile. "Yu' usual table?" So he was a regular, Kelee noted, and relaxed a bit.

"Thanks, Janet. Two lemonades, please," Tyce said to the hostess. Janet nodded and led them to a table at the far end of the room. Their table offered up a great view of the entire restaurant. It was simply decorated with bright pastel mismatched colored tables and chairs that actually worked. Local art lined the wall, with an array of mini Caribbean flags hanging from the rafters. Soft Caribbean fused jazz played in the background. Tyce assisted her into her seat. Kelee thanked him. He took his seat and handed her his cell phone.

"Make yu' call."

She took the phone. "Thank yu'." Kelee smiled at him and dialed Lori's cell, praying she hadn't turned her phone off. The phone went to voice mail. She frowned and ended the call.

"She's not answerin'?" Tyce inquired.

"She's in a meeting so her phone is off."

A waitress bought them lemonades and menus.

"When does her meetin' end?"

"An hour." Kelee sipped her lemonade and sighed as the refreshing liquid slid down her parched throat.

"So have some lunch an' I'll take yu' to her after."

Kelee looked at him, touched by his kindness. Her stomach rumbled; she knew she couldn't refuse. "Thank yu'. I'll pay yu' back when I meet up with my sister."

"Now I'm offended." He frowned. Kelee felt bad. He had been nothing but helpful, but she still didn't know him.

"Sorry, but I don't know yu'. I just met yu'. Yu've been really nice, but . . ."

"Do me a favor, jus' enjoy the lunch. They have some of the best local dishes here."

Kelee relaxed and smiled at him. "Thanks."

"Yu' welcome." He gave her that infectious smile again. She picked up her menu.

Kelee had the fried fish strips and a salad with another glass of the delicious homemade lemonade. Over lunch she learned that Tyce was a businessman. He owned a pharmacy located downtown and a number of variety stores both uptown and downtown. He traveled a lot, especially to Miami to buy special items for his stores. He was born and raised in St. Pala, but he had attended college in Florida. He held a degree in business from Florida University. Kelee in turn told him of her decorating business in New York, which impressed him.

"I'm havin' a new house built," he told her. "Maybe yu' can decorate it for me?"

Kelee smiled at him. "I'm not in St. Pala that long."

"I could fly yu' in," he said. Kelee looked at him, surprised. "It's hard to find a decent decorator on the island and I'm not 'bout to leave it up to my sister. The woman has really bad taste. Yu' should see what she did to my first house."

Kelee laughed, enjoying his company. He was very charming and amusing. Sean's face suddenly flashed before her. She couldn't wait to see him tonight. There was something so intoxicating about Sean. She wished she knew what it was that drew her to him. Only time with him would give her that answer.

"Yu' OK?" Tyce asked and Kelee looked up at him.

"I should go," she said, pushing her plate away.

"OK." Tyce signaled for the waitress. The waitress came with the bill. He pulled out his wallet and paid her in cash.

"Thanks again," Kelee told him.

"My pleasure." He smiled. He was so nice, which she appreciated.

"Wait here," he said outside the restaurant. "My car is across the street."

She watched him cross the street to the craft market parking lot. Kelee checked her watch; she hoped Lori would be out of her meeting by the time she got there. The sooner they got the theft reported to the cops the better.

A few minutes later a black BMW X5 jeep pulled up. Nice, she thought as he assisted her into the brand new jeep—from the smell of it. The interior was spotless.

"Nice ride," she said, relaxing into the plush seat, snapping her seat belt in place.

"Thanks."

He pulled out into traffic. Kelee told him where Lori was and he headed down the street.

"I really appreciate yu' help," Kelee told Tyce as he came to a stop outside the building. She gazed at him, unbuckling her seat belt.

"Thank yu' for havin' lunch with me." He smiled. "An' be careful next time."

"Thanks, I will."

"Can I have yu' number? I might need yu' for decorating reasons." He looked at her in such an honest way Kelee couldn't tell him no. Plus, he had been a perfect gentleman.

"Sure." Kelee smiled at him. She gave Tyce Lori's house number and her business number in New York before getting out of the jeep. She watched him drive off.

Kelee approached the security guard who sat in a small booth at the entrance of the courtyard. The guard was dressed in a khaki uniform.

Shades shielded his eyes from the glaring sun. She prayed he'd remember her from dropping Lori off.

"Hi, I'm here for Lori DeCosta," she told the guard.

"Go on in." He smiled.

"Thank yu'." Kelee smiled at him and went in. She made her way through the courtyard of the building to the entrance. The courtyard was well kept with a small garden in a circle. Benches were sparsely placed against the far walls. Most of the buildings in that area were colonial style and well kept to maintain their colonial history.

Kelee entered the lobby of the hall. A receptionist sat at a desk just below the wooden staircase. She was thin and pretty with a ready gap-toothed smile.

"Hi, I'm here for Lori."

"Yu' Kelee?" the receptionist asked.

"Yes." She smiled at her.

"Yu' sister waitin' in the lobby." She pointed toward the right.

Kelee thanked the receptionist and headed towards the doors; she hoped Lori hadn't been waiting too long. Kelee headed towards the lobby. She entered and interrupted Lori talking with three other women. Kelee had briefly met the women when she had dropped Lori off earlier. The women reeked of island high society with their upper crust attitudes accentuated by their designer outfits.

"Wha' wrong?" Lori asked, concerned, when she saw the look on Lori's face. The women looked on with interest.

Kelee took a deep breath and started. "I was robbed and yu' car was stolen."

"Oh, my God!" Lori cried, grabbing her hands and looking her over. Yu' a'right?" Lori asked, frightened. Kelee smiled at her, nodding her head.

"Yu' weren't hurt?" Mrs. Jackson asked; she was brown skinned with natural reddish blond hair.

"No," Kelee told her.

"Yu' sure?" Lori's face was filled with worry.

Kelee really didn't want Lori to be worried in her state. "Yes, I'm fine. It's just that my purse was snatched and the car was stolen. Lori, I'm really sorry about the car."

"I don't care about the car." Lori pulled her into her arms, hugging her tightly. Kelee hugged her sister and breathed a sigh of relief.

"This man was nice enough to help."

"Yu' have to be so careful nowadays," Mrs. Wong volunteered; she was tall Asian/black with a short curly Afro and slanted light brown eyes.

"It can be dangerous downtown; yu' have to be very aware," Mrs. Johnson added.

"Let me call the chief," Mrs. Hill, a thin black woman with stunning gray eyes, said, and pulled out her cell phone.

"I'm sorry about the car." Kelee looked at Lori.

"Please, stop with the car. I'm jus' glad yu' OK." Lori squeezed her hand. At that moment Kelee was glad she had her big sister. Everything would be OK.

Mrs. Hill was kind enough to drive them home after reporting the car stolen to her brother, who was the commissioner of police. Mrs. Wong's husband owned a car dealership and informed Lori she could have a car tomorrow until hers was found or replaced. Kelee was grateful for the support system the women offered. She had only seen them as snobby rich women, but they were more like a sisterhood. They supported each other, she could see that now, and was glad Lori had them as friends.

Allan waited anxiously on the veranda as they pulled up to the house. They thanked Mrs. Hill for the ride, getting out of her BMW jeep. Mrs. Hill honked her horn before driving off.

"Yu'all OK?" Allan met them at the gate.

"We're fine," Lori told Allan as he started to fuss over her.

"Wha' happened?" He focused on Kelee.

"I have to sit down," Lori announced. Allan gently led her inside.

With Lori comfortably situated on the sofa Allan turned to Kelee for an answer. Kelee relayed the entire story to him.

"I'm really sorry about the car. I guess I wasn't careful enough."

"Don't worry about the car, it can be replaced.

Yu' safety is more important here," Allan replied so strongly, it made Kelee nervous.

"I'm jus' glad someone was nice enough to help her get back to me," Lori said, rubbing her belly. She looked tired.

"Who helped yu'?" Allan asked. "Some guy name Tyce, he drives a black BMW X5 jeep. Know him? No, describe him?" She did. When she was finished Allan shook his head. "I will be more careful next time," Kelee said.

"His name was Tyce."

Allan suddenly looked curious. Kelee wondered why.

"I will be more careful next time," Kelee insisted.

"Stop scarin' her!" Lori slapped Allan on the arm.

"Sorry, didn't mean to." Allan smiled, which put Kelee at ease.

"Wha' time is it?" Lori asked.

Allan looked at the clock on the wall. "Almost four."

"Tell Nadine to start dinner for me. Sean is comin' to dinner tonight."

"Need me to do anything?" Kelee asked, perking up. She had been anticipating seeing Sean again.

"Yu' don't cook, remember?" Lori reminded her.

Kelee rolled her eyes at her. "Only because yu' did everything, mother-hen."

"Yu' were lazy," Lori teased.

Lori was right; she rarely did any cooking growing up. She didn't mind cleaning up, but she never did take to cooking. She knew the basics, but had never delved too far into it. If she did cook it was something quick and simple like grilled chicken or pasta. She never learned how to make traditional dishes; plus they took too damn long to make as far as she was concerned.

While Lori napped, and Allan retreated to his study, Kelee decided to help out by setting the dining table, after which she took a long cool shower. She was coming out of the shower wrapped in her robe when she ran into a wobbling Lori, rubbing sleep from her eyes.

"Why didn't yu' wake me?"

"Yu' looked so tired."

"Come help me get out of this suit," Lori said, heading into her room. Kelee followed. She helped her sister undress and marveled at Lori's naked pregnant body.

"Wha'?" Lori asked when she caught her staring.

"That belly is huge. Yu' sure yu' due in two months?"

Lori rolled her eyes. "Yes."

"Looks like yu' going to drop sooner than that."

"Don't I wish." Lori groaned.

"Is it that bad?" Kelee asked, concerned with her sister's health and knowing how long it had taken her to actually get pregnant.

"Some days are better than others."

Kelee rubbed her sister's bare belly, smiling.

"Could yu' pull me out some'ting to wear, while I take a quick shower? Sean should be here soon." Lori headed into the master bedroom bathroom.

Kelee couldn't wait to see Sean. In a short time he had made quite an impression on her. She recalled the intense dream she had had about him the other night. The funny thing about the dream was that it was as if she had known him all her life. He felt like a long-last lover to her. Why? She wasn't sure.

Kelee went into Lori's walk-in closet and pulled out a floral print A-line dress. She laid it out on the bed, then pulled out underwear and a pair of flat mules.

Allan entered the room as she was about to leave. "I didn't mean to scare yu' earlier," he started to apologize.

"It's OK. I just need to be more careful next time."

He looked at her as if he wanted to tell her something, but he simply smiled and nodded his head in agreement.

"Are yu' guys in any danger or anything I should be aware of?" Kelee asked. Being politically linked brought some danger. But Allan was the minister of tourism. That job wasn't as dangerous as Sean's. However, if there was someone out there she should be concerned with she wanted to know.

"No, no," Allan told her reassuringly.

She was relieved to hear that. "Good. Well, let me go get ready."

"Sean is downstairs."

"He is?" She couldn't help the excitement in her voice. Allan grinned.

"Yeah, he's havin' a drink on the veranda," Allan told her.

Kelee rushed to her room down the hall to get ready. After lightly moisturizing her body she pulled on a cap-sleeve, snap-front, denim mid-calf dress. She applied light makeup and pulled her hair back into a simple ponytail. Half an hour later she ventured downstairs in search of Sean. When she didn't find him on the veranda, she went back into the house. She found him in the kitchen with Nadine. He was plating the fish they were having for dinner. Nadine was pulling the salad from the refrigerator. She paused in the doorway, taking in the vision of him. He was dressed in a chartreuse shirt, his sleeves rolled up. He wore dark blue slacks. He hadn't shaved, she noted from the five o'clock shadow. Somehow it made him even sexier. Even in the kitchen he looked good. He looked at her, then and a warm smile touched his lips. She blushed under his gaze.

"Need any help?" she asked, moving into the room.

"Thanks." Sean handed her the platter with the delicious-smelling slices of swordfish covered in sautéed onions, scallions, and hot pepper. Kelee took the platter into the dining room, which was just off the kitchen. Lori and Allan entered the room as she placed the platter beside the bowls of fresh vegetables and rice.

"I'll get the punch." Allan went into the kitchen. Kelee helped Lori into her chair, before sitting beside her.

"I see yu' glad he's here," Lori whispered. Kelee shushed her just as Sean and Allan walked into the dining room. Allan sat at the head of the table. Sean sat to Allan's left, across from Lori and Kelee. Their eyes met and held and he smiled at her. Kelee suddenly felt flushed.

The conversation around the dinner table was light and entertaining until Allan mentioned Kelee getting robbed earlier. A look of dread came over Sean's face as he focused on her. She was struck by the intense concern on his face.

"Yu' sure yu' OK?" Sean's eyes searched hers. She couldn't help being curious by his concern. He really didn't know her enough to be this intensely concerned.

"Yes, I'm fine. All he did was grab my purse, which unfortunately had Lori's car keys in it."

"Would yu' be able to recognize him, if yu' saw him again?"

"No, all I saw was his back," Kelee told him.

"Are yu' sure?" Sean pressed. Kelee suddenly felt uneasy with his questioning. She'd forgotten he was a cop.

"Sean!" Lori warned. Sean looked at Lori and his intense expression disappeared.

"Sorry, I didn't mean to alarm yu'."

Kelee looked from Sean to Lori to Allan. Was she missing something here? "What's going on?"

"No'ting," Lori started. "These two love to exaggerate 'tings too much. I was robbed once. Yu' jus' have to be very aware when yu' go downtown, that's all," Lori said sternly.

Kelee looked at her sister, alarmed. She had never told her that. "Yu' were robbed?" Kelee asked.

"My purse was snatched; luckily a cop saw it all and caught the guy. Now can we change the subject?" Lori was getting upset and no one wanted that. They went back to enjoying the dinner.

"Keep next weekend free," Allan told Sean.

"Why?" Sean asked.

"The Appleton Rum party in View Coast," Allan told Sean. "Yu' are comin', right?"

"I could use some R&R," Sean admitted, looking at Kelee. She pressed her lips together, preventing the smile that threatened to show.

View Coast was a resort area where tourists flocked. It was also the playground for St. Pala's elite. Kelee had to admit that it was exciting to know that Sean was going to be in View Coast for that weekend. Lori had told her about the weekend excursion, which she had been looking forward to. Having Sean there would make it a lot more enjoyable. She recalled the last time she was in View Coast and her memorable affair with a young dreadlock name Mike. But that was ten years ago; she was young and desperate to get rid of her virginity at the time. Which was kind of stupid, she had to admit. But she was young and immature in those days. Plus, her wild days were long over, or were they? she wondered as she looked at Sean St. John. The man was sexy and fine as hell and all she could think of was how he'd be in bed. As if sensing her thoughts he turned and his eyes met and held hers, promising her satisfaction to her thoughts. Kelee looked away, embarrassed by her thoughts and Sean seeming to know what she was thinking.

Just before dessert, Lori complained about feeling a bit tired, so Allan took her upstairs.

"Nadine made cake for dessert," Kelee told Sean.

"Let me take yu' out for dessert?" Sean suggested. The way he said dessert told her that he had more than food on his mind. She concealed a smile that threatened to surface.

"That sounds good," she responded cooly.

Moments later they were in his jeep and

heading down the hill. He maneuvered his jeep around a bend. The other side of the road offered a beautiful view of homes cascading down the hillside and the lights of downtown in the distance.

"Are yu' sure yu' not married with kids somewhere?"

He laughed before responding. "Yes."

"Yu' sure? I wouldn't want some crazed baby mother coming after me."

"Yu' don't have any'ting to worry 'bout," he reassured her with a smile.

"So tell me why yu' don't have a woman, again?"

"Again?" He gazed briefly at her, hiding a smile.

"Yes."

"Because I don't like to get involved with a woman—not unless I really like her or want to be with her. I don't like to waste my time, do yu'?"

His answer wasn't exactly what she expected to hear. She didn't know how to respond.

"Do yu'?" he asked again.

"No, no," Kelee responded, gazing at him. She was really starting to like him. He was straightforward and she liked that in a man. She had been lied to enough by the men in her past. An honest man was welcome.

"But yu' do know that I'm here for a short time?"

"I know. An' I intend to make the best of it."
He gave her an infectious smile.

Sean took her to a restaurant/bar called
Haven. Haven was a house in a valley surrounded by a thriving garden. It was one of the
exclusive hot spots that couples frequented.

The hostess, a pretty white woman, greeted
them. Sean told her he wanted a deck table
and she led them around a path illuminated by
tea-tree lights at the back of the house. A large
deck extended from the back of the house.
Small intimate candlelit tables created a ro-
mantic setting. Couples were scattered about the
deck. A part of the deck served as a dance floor
where three couples were locked in an intimate
embrace. The night air was cool with the fresh
scent of flowers from the gardens.

They were seated at a small table where they
could see into the dining area. It was just as intimate with candlelit tables.

"This place is great," she said, taking in the intricate details of the glass candle on their table.

"Thank yu'." He smiled at her and she paused,
looking at him.

"Yu' own it?" She was surprised.

"Yes, but I keep it a secret." He grinned.

"Why?" she asked, curious.

"In my line of work, the less people know
about me the better."

The waitress came over to take their order.

"What do yu' suggest?" she asked him. His hazel eyes smiled at her.

He ordered the mama's cake for both of them. She ordered a white wine and he ordered a Heineken.

"Mama's cake?" she asked, curious.

"My mother perfected the recipe. It was passed down from her great-great grandmother. Haven is well known for her cake."

"Where is yu' mother?"

"Miami. She and my father moved there to be with my sisters and their grandchildren," he responded gently.

"Sounds like yu' miss them." She noted his solemn expression.

"I jus' came back from Miami a few weeks ago."

"So all yu' immediate family is in Miami?"

"Yeah."

"Ever think of relocating?"

"No, I love St. Pala too much." He smiled. She could see he did. He was devoted to his island and his people to the point that he had chosen to protect them. She couldn't help but admire him.

The waitress arrived with their dessert and drinks. Mama's cake was absolutely delicious, it was a layered cake filled with mixed fruit accented by a hint of liquor.

"This is really good," she said between bites.

"I knew yu'd like it." Sean nodded as he ate his cake.

"My compliments to yu' mother."

"I'll pass on the compliment," he said, pushing his empty plate aside and reaching for his beer.

A slow reggae tune came on and she started to rock to the tune. "Dance with me?" she asked.

He smiled and obliged. They moved out onto the dance floor, where Sean pulled her close into an intimate embrace. The heat and the smooth musk scent of his cologne filled her senses as she pressed her body into his muscular frame. She wrapped her arms around his neck, resting her head on his shoulder. His arms circled her waist, one resting just above her rear as he held her close. They moved to the music, allowing the smooth rhythm to flow over them. A sense of belonging washed over her. He felt right, too right. He was starting to evoke feelings within her that scared her. His hand caressed her back, molding her into him. She closed her eyes, giving in to the safe, soothing feel of him. His hand moved up to caress the back of her neck. He gently pulled her head off his shoulders. She gazed at him, opening her eyes. The look in his eyes took her breath away. He wanted her and it was all there in his eyes. The blatant knowledge of it sent shivers down her spine. Kelee couldn't deny the fact that she wanted him, too. Her heart raced at the thought, the possibility of being with him in the most intimate way. He lowered his head to hers and Kelee closed her eyes as his lips covered hers in a slow heated kiss. Her senses went wild with the feel, the taste of him. Gently Sean's lips and tongue caressed her lips until they parted. She welcomed the smooth invasion of his tongue. She moaned softly, tightening her arms about his neck. Kelee caressed his tongue with her own, loving the taste of him. For how long they danced and kissed, she didn't know. The song changed, and they pulled back, gazing into each other's eyes. There was an undeniable connection between them. Kelee's heart raced with excitement. Sean St. John was a man she couldn't deny. What she was feeling was far too intense. He pulled her back into his arm and they resumed their dance. Kelee laid her head on his shoulder, closing her eyes.

They went back to their table at the end of the song to finish their drinks. Sean pulled his chair close to her, cuddling her in his arms as she sipped the last of her wine. Their conversation turned to their likes and dislikes. Kelee found out that they loved swimming, movies, and sightseeing. They talked about their families and being apart from them and the strain it caused at times.

"Wha' do yu' like?" Sean asked, caressing the back of her neck.

"In general or in a man?" She gazed at him.

"A man," he said.

"Honesty and respect is key."

He looked at her deeply, as if mesmerized by her words.

"An' if a man can't be honest right away, for some unknown reason?"

"As long as he comes clean at some point, it's good." She smiled.

"I'm gonna hold yu' to yu' word."

"Yu' got something to tell me?" she asked cautiously.

"Not yet," he teased, kissing her lightly.

"As long as it's not bad," she whispered against his lips.

"Trust me, it's not." He caressed her ear, sending shivers down her spine. "Come; let's go," he whispered. Kelee simply followed him.

Tyce watched Sean and Kelee drive away from the Haven. He was seated in his car at the far end of the parking lot, hidden from sight. He had been following Sean all day unnoticed. Tyce prided himself on his surveillance technique. He pulled out his cell phone and hit speed dial. His boss answered the phone on the second ring.

"She's good," he told the boss.

"Good; yu' know what to do."

Tyce ended the call. He started his car and pulled out of the parking lot, heading home for some much needed sleep.

* * *

Sean drove Kelee back to Lori's house. They didn't say much, as they simply enjoyed each other's company. At the house, Sean walked her into the dark living room, a sure sign that Allan and Lori had retired for the night.

"When can I see yu' again?" Kelee asked, turning to face Sean. Sean immediately pulled her into his arms, kissing her until her senses were spinning out of control and she was breathless. She clung to him, wanting more than his kisses. She wanted him to make love to her. She needed to feel him inside her. The severity of her thoughts shocked and excited her.

"Is the guest room empty?" he asked, referring to the room just off the washroom to the back of the house.

"Yes," she whispered and felt her entire body tremble with excitement. In one swoop he lifted her and took her down the hall to the guest room. Inside the small room with only a twin bed and a dresser, he placed her in the middle of the bed, coming down on her. She moaned, wrapping her arms about his neck. His mouth covered hers in a scorching kiss. He unsnapped the top of her dress, exposing her pink bra. He pushed her bra off her shoulder, exposing her left breast, which he covered with his hot mouth. She moaned, crying out his name as he suckled her hungrily. He pulled back briefly and with one quick move he unsnapped her entire dress, exposing her hot flesh. His eyes devoured her body and a pleasant smile curled his lips. She loved the way his eyes made love to her body. He reached down and cupped her through her panties and she moaned loudly. He applied pressure, caressing her through the thin lace. He covered her breast, suckling her. She gripped his head, arching her back, opening her legs more. She felt his harden sex rise up against her thigh. His fingers found their way under her pink panties and into her wet folds. She pulled his head up to her, kissing him hungrily. His fingers sank farther between her folds and inside. The sweet invasion took her breath away. She couldn't think straight or even hear what he had said to her. He stopped his sensuous assault on her. She opened her eyes, looking at him.

"Do yu' have protection?" he asked.

"No," she whispered, catching her breath.

"No'ting upstairs?" he asked, his hand working in small circles against her. She moaned, closing her eyes. She didn't want him to stop.

"No," she told him, breathless as his fingers moved in and out of her with delicious slowness. She felt the tightness start in her toes and work its way up to her breasts.

"Too bad," he continued and lowered his head back to her breast, gently biting at her nipples as his fingers quickened their pace. Kelee thrust her hips into his hands, praying he wouldn't stop.

"Don't stop," she cried.

"I don't intend to—at least not this." He covered her mouth with his tongue, mimicking the movement of his fingers. He was driving her crazy. She felt her body peak and her senses exploded into a million stars.

"Yu' wicked." She smiled, opening her eyes.

"At least yu' know wha' to expect when we do this the right way," he told her, caressing her breasts. She caressed his face, looking deeply into his eyes, wondering why he felt so right to her. He kissed her lightly as he sat up, pulling her up with him.

"I can't wait," she moaned.

"Neither can I." He kissed her long and hard before saying good night.

Chapter 6

Kelee's dreams were filled of Sean that night. In her dreams they had made endless love. She woke with a huge smile on her face, recalling how Sean had her, literally, melting in his hands last night. She couldn't wait to be with him, but the first thing she needed to do was buy some damn condoms. She was impressed with him respecting her by not going any farther other than pleasing her with those magic fingers of his. It showed a sense of responsibility, which she respected him for.

After lingering in bed with thoughts of Sean, Kelee finally ventured downstairs for breakfast. She found Lori on the back veranda, sipping tea. She poured herself a cup of coffee and joined her.

"Allan's off already?" Kelee asked, pulling up a chair. The late morning air was cool with a light breeze. The skies were a bit overcast with the promise of rain.

"Yeah; so how was dessert?" Lori asked with a wicked grin.

"Enjoyable." Kelee couldn't help but smile.

"Yu' give him some?" Lori asked, excited.

"Almost did," she admitted.

"So wha' happen?"

"No protection," Kelee said.

Lori nodded her head in approval. "Told yu' he was different."

"There's something so familiar about him." Kelee recalled the sense of being so comfortable with Sean.

"Wha' do yu' mean?" Lori asked, curious.

"It's like I know him."

"That's good, isn't it?"

"Yes, but it's really strange. He's so familiar, like I've known him before."

"Yu' two made a connection, that's good." Lori smiled.

"I guess, but I can't shake this feeling of knowing him."

"It was almost like that with Allan an' me. It was instant, we both knew it."

"That must be it." Kelee sighed and sipped her coffee. "It's just so strange connecting to someone so quickly. Yu' know how long it takes for me to really trust someone."

"I know but sometimes yu' just have to let 'tings happen."

"Yu' right," Kelee admitted, looking at the

clouds as they rolled in. She heard the roar of a distant thunder.

"He does understand that yu'll be going back to New York?" Lori asked. Kelee could hear the concern in her voice.

"Yes, we talked about that."

"An'?" Lori pressed.

"He understands," Kelee told Lori. However, she couldn't help but wonder if getting involved with Sean was a good idea. She couldn't deny the fact that she wanted him. She knew he felt the same; last night had proved that. There was some level of danger in getting involved with Sean, regardless of their mutual attraction. She had to be careful not to fall for him. Men like Sean were easy to fall for, which made them a danger to any woman with an open heart. She had to guard her heart well against him. She took some comfort in the fact that he understood their situation and was comfortable with it.

Sean sat at his desk reminiscing about Kelee. He loved the way her body had responded to him last night. He couldn't wait to make love to her. He wanted to feel her wrapped around him. He wanted to hear her cry out his name. Last night he knew he had put his mark on her. She would have given in to him regardless of the condom issue. He laughed under his breath because last night he did have a condom.

He wanted to make sure that she really wanted him and she did. His plan to seduce her was going along just fine.

"I see she still have yu' smilin'; must be nice," Jack said, entering his office. Sean pushed all thoughts of Kelee aside.

"Wha' yu' have for me?"

"Yu' not goin' to tell me who she is?" Jack asked.

"No," he insisted.

"Mus' be good." Jack grinned.

"Can we move on?" he asked, pretending to be annoyed.

Jack laughed. "Now I can't wait to meet her."

Sean glared at him and Jack got serious, briefing him on a potential bad situation involving some deportees who were actually from Africa looking to start up a drug ring.

"Put Hall and King on it; the minute they do some'ting I want them locked up," Sean told Jack.

Deportees were the leading cause of violence in the Caribbean these days. Many of them were too embarrassed to be deported to their native island so they told the U.S.A., Canada, and England immigration that they were from other islands. Many of them were starting to create gangs, causing violence to escalate on some islands. Jamaica was having a big problem right now with its deportees. Sean wasn't about to have any of it—not in St. Pala. The minute they did something illegal he was locking them up for good.

"Wha' 'bout Mike?" he asked.

"He's still in Cayman."

"I want to know the minute he sets foot back here," Sean insisted.

"Yu' got it." Jack nodded.

"No'ting on Adams and Penn?"

"No'ting'. I'm runnin' out of 'tings to tell the families," Jack told him.

"Tell them they had to go to Cayman to do an investigation." Sean was grasping at straws and they both knew it. Jack gave him a questioning look. He also knew that Adams' and Penn's wives wouldn't buy it, but it was all he had to give right now. He had run out of places to look for them; it was like they had disappeared into thin air. Sean had to keep the faith. He wouldn't believe anything until he saw his men, dead or alive, preferably alive.

"Yu' sure yu' want to do that?"

"Jus' tell them." He sighed, frustrated. He didn't want to give them anything to worry about when he didn't have any proof.

Jack left his office. Sean sat in silence listening to the rain beat against the air-conditioner unit in the window. He needed to find his men. He had exhausted just about all his possibilities, but there were still a few people he could call, so he got on the phone.

Sean spent a great part of his day on the

phone. By the time he had gotten home he was drained. As he relaxed with a Red Stripe beer, his thoughts drifted to Kelee. He picked up the phone.

Lori answered the phone on the third ring. "Hello?"

"Hey, baby mama," he teased, and Lori laughed.

"Keep it up," Lori warned, amused.

"How yu' feelin', by the way?" he asked on a more serious note. She was on the last leg of her pregnancy and he knew it wasn't always pleasant. He had heard enough stories from his sisters to know.

"Not too bad," Lori told him.

"Good."

"Yu' want to talk to Kelee?" she asked before he could say anything else.

"That would be nice." He smiled.

"She's in the shower; want her to call yu' back?" Lori asked.

"Yeah." He closed his eyes, allowing the tension of the day to flow out of his body.

"Where are yu'?"

"At the house."

"Yu' sound tired."

"I am," he admitted.

"She's startin' to like yu'," Lori said and a sense of guilt washed over Sean. He had the utmost respect for Lori. She was like family. He wondered what she would think of him when she found out what he was doing to her sister. He wondered if Lori really knew what her sister was like back then. How she had used him, then left him without so much as a good-bye. He intended to make Kelee regret what she had done to him.

"Yu' still there?" Lori asked, pulling him back to the present.

"Yeah," he said, clearing his throat.

"Yu' OK?" The concern in Lori's question made him feel guilty, but he pushed the feeling aside. There was no time for guilt; he was sure Kelee never regretted what she did to him back then.

"Yeah. Tell her to call me?" he said in a cheerful tone.

"OK. Good night," Lori told him.

"Night," he said and hung up the phone.

A part of Sean knew what he was doing wasn't right, but he couldn't stop now. He couldn't just come out and tell her who he really was. He would see this game to the end. Sean got another beer and waited for her call.

"Mornin'," Kelee greeted Lori and Allan as she entered the kitchen. They were seated at the dining table.

"Mornin'," they said in unison.

Kelee joined them at the table for a hearty breakfast of fried sweet plantains, thin slices of honey ham, scrambled eggs, and toast. Nadine bought her a cup of coffee, as Kelee loaded up her plate. Her morning breakfast usually consisted of a yogurt, coffee, and maybe a muffin depending on how hungry she was.

"Oh, by the way, Sean called for yu' last night," Lori told her.

Kelee paused. "He did?"

"Yeah, he wanted yu' to call him back, but yu' were asleep by the time I got upstairs," Lori said.

"Oh," she moaned, disappointed.

"His house number is by the phone, but I doubt he's home. I'll give yu' his cell."

"I don't want to disturb him, especially if he's at work." Kelee reached for another slice of ham.

"I don't think he'll mind." Allan grinned. Kelee blushed, hiding a smile.

Sean was just about to get into his jeep when his cell phone rang. He pulled it from his hip, glanced at the number and smiled.

"Hello," he answered, leaning against the door of the jeep.

"Hi," Kelee's soft sultry voice came over the line. He'd been expecting her call. He had fallen asleep on the sofa, waiting to hear from her last night.

"I've been expectin' yu' call," he told her.

"Sorry. Lori just gave me yu' message. I was asleep by the time Lori came upstairs."

"Dream of me?" he teased and she laughed.

"Maybe," she teased back.

"Hope it was good." He grinned.

"Like I'd tell yu'." Her voice was laced with amusement.

"Yu' wouldn't?" He pretended to be hurt.

"Yu' busy?"

"Not right now," he told her.

"So when can I see yu'?"

"I have a meetin', but I'll be free after three. I could pick yu' up around four."

"Where are yu' taking me?"

"Don't know yet."

"I just wanted to know how to dress."

"Any'ting' yu' wear is fine," he told her, getting into his jeep.

"OK, four then?"

"Yu' got it." He smiled. He had to admit that it pleased him that she wanted to see him. She was an intoxicating, beautiful woman who was easy to talk to and be with. He recalled her telling how familiar he was to her and the tinge of guilt that came over him then. He had managed to keep his emotions in check at that moment. In good time he would reveal who he really was, but for now he had to make sure he maintained her interest.

Kelee must have changed outfits at least six times before she settled on jeans, a rayon wrapped shirt, and mules. She asked Lori to do her hair in a single braid down her back.

"So where's he takin' yu'?" Lori asked.

"Don't know," Kelee said, excited.

"Yu' really like him?"

"Yeah," she admitted. "Is there something I should know about him?" she asked, concerned.

"No, Sean's a good man."

"But?" Kelee waited for her to continue.

"I jus' don't want to see yu' end up hurt. Women fall so easily for him, and he knows it. He's not conceited or anything like that, but he does have them falling at his feet."

Kelee told her, "Don't worry about me, I can take care of myself."

"I know that, but how will yu' handle walkin' away from him when yu' have to leave?"

"I'll handle it," Kelee reassured her with a smile.

"Yu' sure?" Lori looked at her, concerned.

"Yes, Mommy." She laughed and kissed Lori's cheek.

Sean picked her up a few minutes after four. As always, he looked good. He was a bit wrinkled and sweaty, but still, he looked good.

"We have to stop at my house so I can take a shower before we go; is that OK? Or I could swing back and pick yu' up in an hour."

"No, I'll come with yu'. I'd like to see yu'

house," she told him and got a smile that took her breath away.

"Thought yu' might." He grinned and helped her into his jeep.

At the top of the road Kelee noted that he headed farther uphill. She took note of the luxury homes on their way up. She was surprised when a few minutes later he pulled up to the gate of a massive house.

"Yu' live here?" she asked when he pressed a control that opened the gate.

"Yes. Yu' like it?" he asked.

"Are yu' joking?" Kelee asked as he drove down the path towards an open garage.

Kelee got out of the jeep following Sean, marveling at the beauty of his two-level house. She loved the endless veranda and the soft cream and blue. She paused and turned to look out from the house and was met with the spectacular view of homes cascading down the hill. She spotted Lori's house and immediately turned to find Sean grinning at her.

"Great view." She studied him as he casually leaned against the railing.

"It is." His eyes were focused on her, making her blush.

"Come in." He gestured towards the richly detailed front door of mahogany and stained glass. She followed him into the foyer; cream decorative tile gleamed under the lights. End tables held fresh flowers. A curved wooden stairwell led to the upstairs. The man had a great sense of style. He definitely knew how to decorate. She followed him into the living room, and instantly fell in love with his Caribbean colonial styled furniture.

"Did yu' have yu' furniture custom made?" she asked, taking a closer look at the intricate carvings on the wall unit that held delicate mini statues. She admired a crystal market vendor woman, sitting over her basket of fruits.

"These are exquisite, yu' have really good taste," she said, impressed. She touched the cool crystal of the statue.

"Thanks," he replied in a sarcastic tone. Kelee turned to look at him.

"I didn't mean it like that." She pursed her lips. He had a playful smile on his face.

"Did yu' use a decorator?"

"No," he told her.

"Yu' have good taste," she complimented him.

"Thanks." He smiled. "Let me go shower and change. Feel free to look around."

"OK," she said, excited about seeing what he had done to the rest of the house.

Kelee explored the rest of the downstairs. There was a sitting/TV room that housed a huge TV, plush couches, and a bar. There was also a small library, with a computer set up in one corner. She loved his spacious kitchen. The dining room sat just off the kitchen. The one thing she noted was how spotless his house was;

he definitely had a housekeeper. She turned to leave the kitchen and gasped when she saw a very serious-looking middle-aged woman, arms crossed, glaring at her.

"Hi," she greeted the woman with a smile. The woman glared even harder at her. Kelee suddenly wondered if she should make a run for it. The woman was blocking the doorway, so that exit was out.

"Who yu'?" the woman asked in a gentle voice. Kelee relaxed a bit.

"Kelee, a friend of Sean's," she told her.

The woman's face relaxed a bit and she nodded. Kelee felt a little better. The woman was truly intimidating, with her hard leathery face and mean scowl. "Oh. Where is he?"

"Showering. He told me I could look around."

"Yu' want some'ting to drink?" the woman offered, moving to a cupboard and opening the door, pulling out a glass.

"Thank yu'. What's yu' name, if I may ask?" Kelee asked carefully, wondering who she was.

The woman paused and studied her for a moment before responding. "May Brown, housekeeper."

Kelee smiled and moved towards her with her hand out. "Nice to meet yu'," Kelee told her. May simply looked at her hand. Kelee dropped her hand.

"Wha' yu' want to drink?"

"Juice is good." Kelee watched her. Apparently

May wasn't all that friendly, but she was nice enough to offer her a drink. So, she couldn't be all that bad.

Kelee watched her as she poured her some juice from a jug. She offered it to Kelee, who took it, thanking her with a smile and taking a sip. The juice was different, but delicious.

"Mmmm, this is good, what is it?" Kelee smiled at her.

"Passion fruit, pineapple and ginger, Sean's favorite," May said with a slight smile.

Kelee drank some more. "Delicious. Thank yu'."

"Which island yu' from?"

Kelee stopped drinking and told her, "Jamaica."

"Knew a Jamaican man once," May mused with a reflective look in her eyes. "Nice man." She shrugged. Kelee couldn't help but smile. She found May's subtle expressions amusing.

"How long have yu' worked for Sean?"

"Five years," May told her.

"What's he like as a boss? He doesn't overwork yu', does he?" Kelee smiled at her with curiosity. May smiled, flashing perfect white dentures. Her smile lessened the harshness in her face.

"He's a good boss." May regarded her with a curious expression. "Yu' mus' be special."

Kelee was surprised by May's words.

"Why do yu' say that?" Kelee was curious about the meaning behind her statement.

"He never brings anyone home."

May's answer stunned Kelee; for a moment she wasn't sure if she should be flattered or cautious.

She was about to press May for more information when she heard footsteps. She turned to see Sean entering the kitchen. He was dressed in jeans and a cream polo shirt. His hair was still wet but he looked so good, Kelee couldn't help but stare at him. He smiled at them.

"Talkin' 'bout me?"

"Maybe," Kelee teased.

"It better be good," he said with a sexy smirk. He looked at the glass in her hand and said, "Good, my favorite."

May moved to get him a glass and poured him some juice. Kelee watched him as he drank the entire contents. May flashed a knowing grin.

"Ready?" Sean moved to put his glass in the sink.

"Yes," she told him.

May took her glass from her. "Thank yu'."

May nodded at her.

"Let's go," Sean said, putting an arm about her waist.

"How come yu' never bought anyone home?" Kelee asked Sean as they headed down the hill.

"Wha'?" Sean asked, stunned.

"May said yu' never bring anyone home."

His rich laugh filled the jeep, making her smile.

"She mus' have taken a like-in' to yu'," Sean said.

"Is that good or bad?" Kelee was curious.

"It's good." He smiled at her. Kelee was flattered.

Chapter 7

"Where are we going?" Kelee asked. They were heading into the district area uptown.

"A friend of mine is having a birthday bash at the Swan," he said, maneuvering through traffic around Kings Circle.

"Isn't the Swan one of the hottest nightclubs in St. Pala?"

"Yeah."

"Am I dressed OK?" she asked, gazing at him.

"Yu' always dressed jus' right." He smiled, reaching over to caress her thigh. She blushed.

The Swan's parking lot was almost packed when they arrived. Sean found a tight spot and pulled into it. He took her hand as they walked across the lot to the club. The club's exterior was a replica of an Oriental temple. The bouncer, a large mass of a man, greeted Sean warmly before letting them inside. Music bounced off the walls of the red and gold room. The dance floor was packed with birthday wishers having a great time. Sean led her through a sea of people—some he stopped to shake hands with. Finally they made it over to the DJ booth where four men were. The thickest one in the bunch came forward to hug Sean.

"Happy birthday, an' don't look for a present," Sean told him.

"Yu' sure?" the man asked, looking right at her. Kelee smiled at him.

"Hell, no!" Sean pulled her close.

"We always share." The man winked at her.

"Happy birthday," Kelee told him.

"Thank yu', sweetness, what's yu' name?"

"Kelee, and yu'?"

"Jay." Jay looked at Sean. "Yu' betta' hold on to her tight," he warned, looking back at her.

"Trust me, I intend to," Sean responded, tightening his hold on her. Kelee smiled at him.

Just then a pretty pint-size woman with natural short hair moved up to Jay. Jay smiled down at her.

"Sean, how yu' doin', long time no see." She smiled. Sean released her to hug and kiss the woman's cheek.

"I know," Sean said before pulling her back against him. The woman looked at her.

"Penny, Kelee. Kelee, Penny, Jay's wife." Sean introduced them. Penny smiled at Kelee, who returned the smile.

Jay smiled down at Penny, pulling her close to him.

"Was he flirtin' again?" Penny asked, gazing up at Jay.

"He always is," Sean said. Jay rolled his eyes, laughing. Penny poked Jay in the side with her elbow.

"Not because it's yu' birthday. Yu' goin' to behave," Penny warned.

"Why yu' killin' my joy, woman?" Jay asked in a serious tone, but his eyes sparkled with mischief.

"Yu' want to lose a limb tonight?" Penny asked with a smile. Jay laughed and pulled his wife close, kissing the top of her head.

Kelee looked at Sean.

"Don't worry, they do this all the time," Sean whispered to her.

"But I can misbehave with yu' later, right?" Jay asked with a twinkle in his eyes.

"Yu' got that right." Penny grinned.

"My kinda' woman." Jay beamed.

"Are yu' two done?" Sean asked.

"We jus' startin'," Jay sang and dragged his wife out onto the dance floor.

"They seem fun," Kelee said.

"They're good friends," he told her. "Come, let me get yu' some'ting to drink.

Sean found them a small table in the VIP section, then went to get some drinks.

Kelee was checking out the crowd and bobbing

her head to the music when someone tapped her on the shoulder. She looked up to see Tyce.

"Hi." She smiled at him. He sat down across from her.

"Good to see yu'," he said with a smile. "How yu' doin'?"

"Good, thanks."

"Yu' not here alone are yu'?"

"No," she told him with a smile.

"Lucky man. Well, enjoy, hope to see yu' again."

"OK," she told him and watched him disappear into the crowd.

Moments later Sean returned with their drinks. "Who was that?" he asked as he sat down.

"Tyce, the man who came to my rescue," she told him, sipping her drink.

"Oh," Sean said, looking out into the crowd.

"Yu' know him?" Kelee asked, curious.

"No." He focused on her. "Yu' lookin' forward to the weekend?"

"Definitely, as long as yu' there." She smiled. Two nights of music, good food and some of the best drinks; she was looking forward to the weekend. Plus, the beaches of the west coast were spectacular; she couldn't wait to get into the water.

"I'll be there," he said with a knowing smirk that promised a lot. She couldn't help but wonder what he had planned. Whatever it was, she was looking forward to it.

A popular dance hall tune came on and the entire place erupted in a cheer. Sean dragged her out onto the crowed dance floor where everyone was grinding on each other. Sean pulled her close and they started to grind to the music, like everyone else. Kelee pressed her body into Sean, wrapping her arms around his neck, their faces inches from each other.

Tyce took note of the way Sean was looking at Kelee. He stood on the upper level of the club looking down at them dancing. They made a very beautiful couple, he had to admit. They really liked each other. He could see it in the way they looked at each other. She was the perfect weapon of choice. He watched as Sean's hand moved down to Kelee's behind. She had such a great body. He envied Sean at that moment because he was able to touch her, but he also knew the boss had other plans for her. His time would come.

Kelee felt the vibration against her hip and pulled back, looking at Sean.

"Sorry," he said and reached for his phone. He looked at the caller ID and his face went serious. "I have to step outside for a minute," he told her. "Yu' wanna' wait at the table for me?"

"I could use some fresh air, it is warm in here," she said. Dancing with him had her sweating.

"OK." He smiled at her. He took her hand

and led her through the sea of people. The cool night air was welcoming as she stepped outside.

He was on his phone the instant they were outside.

"Where are yu'?" he asked the person on the line. "Swan's . . . I'll wait," he said and ended his call, looking at her.

"Duty calls?" she asked, a bit disappointed.

He gave her an apologetic look. "The night isn't over yet," he said. She hoped he was right because it was starting to seem like every time they were together he had to run off to do something.

"This shouldn't take too long," he started but stopped as a jeep pulled into the lot and up to them. A striking man with the most amazing green eyes stepped out. He was intimidating in both stature and looks.

"Lex called," the man told Sean. "He wouldn't talk to me."

"Now?" Sean asked, frustrated.

"He wouldn't tell me any'ting," the man responded, looking at her.

"Jack, this is Kelee. Kelee, Jack, my partner," Sean introduced them.

"Nice to finally meet yu'." Jack's smile widened.

"Nice to meet yu', too," Kelee told him.

"Where's Lex now?" Sean asked.

"At his old water hole," Jack told him.

"I need yu' to take Kelee to my apartment," Sean said and Kelee looked at him, alarmed. "I promise I won't be long." He smiled at her, squeezing her hand. "Jack will keep yu' company," he reassured her and she relaxed somewhat. This wasn't exactly how she wanted to spend her night. She was sure that Jack was a nice man, but he wasn't whom she wanted to spend her evening with. But she would make the best of it; Sean had promised her that the night wasn't over; she would hold on to that.

Kelee watched disappointed as Sean got into his jeep and drove off. Jack assisted her into his jeep and they drove out of the parking lot.

"Does Sean have any'ting to eat at his apartment?" she asked.

"Don't know," Jack told her.

"Can I pick up some'ting to eat?"

"Sure, wha' yu' feel like?" Jack said, stopping at a light.

"Any good jerk pork around here?" she asked; she hadn't had any since she'd been here last.

"Yeah, I know a lady who makes the best jerk in New Pala," Jack told her, making a U-turn.

"How long have yu' and Sean been partners?" she asked, gazing at Jack.

"Since we entered the academy together."

"That long?" She was impressed.

"Yeah, he's like family," Jack said as he came to a stop outside a small shack/shop painted a bright orange and red, with pictures of all different type of steaming pots. Reggae boomed from large speakers outside the shop. Just outside the doors, small plastic tables and chairs were set up. Hungry patrons enjoyed jerk and drinks at the tables. The patrons, mostly men, paused to gaze at her as Jack led her inside the shack. Inside, a couple waited to be served. The aroma was wonderful, filled with the scent of fish, meat, and spice. The serving counter was wood and held a display case with fried fish, dumplings, and bami—a flat cake made of cassava, and sugar logs, deep fried. A short swinging door separated the kitchen area. Kelee could see a woman and two men with caps working in the back. The woman came out with a Styrofoam container. She bagged it and handed it to the couple waiting. The woman looked at Jack and smiled.

"Hey, Jack, how yu' doin'?" she asked with a gap-toothed smile. She then looked at Kelee with curiosity.

"She's Sean's, so don't start," Jack warned and the woman laughed.

"So, what can I get yu'?" the woman asked.

"Pork, and wheat bread if yu' have any," Kelee told her.

"One servin' or two?" she asked, looking at Jack.

"One pork for her, and chicken for me," Jack said.

The woman smiled and went into the back. A few minutes later she came out with their order.

"Wha' yu' want to drink?" Jack asked her.

Kelee looked at the shelf of drinks that they

offered. "I'll take the large coconut water, no pulp," she told the woman. Jack paid for their meal and they left. Kelee couldn't wait to get to her food.

"Yu' can start eatin' if yu' want," Jack told her.

"No, I'll wait until I get to Sean's place," she said, as she cradled the food on her lap. Jack drove them to a gated apartment complex. The security guard recognized Jack and let them in. Kelee gazed up at the ten-level apartment complex. She could tell from the gated security and the expensive cars on the lot that it was costly to live here. She wondered why Sean would have an apartment here when he had such a big house. Then again, in his line of work and the time it took to get up the hill to his house, he probably needed a place closer to the city. The lobby of the building was bright and painted a cool yellow. They took the elevator to the sixth floor. Jack led her down the hall towards apartment 6D. Jack opened the door and she followed him in. The apartment was spacious with a large room, serving as both living room and dining area. It was sparsely decorated with a large sofa and matching recliner, an end table and a coffee table. The dining area, which was right off the kitchen, held a simple oak table with four chairs. Kelee noted the bare walls. French doors led out onto a small deck. The place was clean, she noted.

"He doesn't spend much time here, does he?"

Kelee asked, pulling their food out of the bag. Jack took his marked container.

"Yu' can tell?" Jack pulled off a couple of paper towel sheets from the dispenser on the counter and handed one to her. They moved over to the dining table.

"No plants, no paintings on the wall, nothing special, unlike his house." She opened her container; the scent of the food was welcoming, and it looked so good.

"So yu've been to his house." Jack smiled. Kelee gazed at him, curious.

"Sean doesn't take anyone he doesn't like to his house. Yu' must be special."

"Why yu' say that?"

"Sean doesn't get too close to people. Don't get me wrong, he's friendly, but he's also very private."

"So yu' never met any of his females?"

Jack looked at her and grinned. "Yu' know it wouldn't be right for me to put his business out there like that," he said.

Kelee knew he was right. She was butting into Sean's business far too early. She buried the many questions she had about him and ate a piece of the pork. It was really good.

"This is good," she said between bites. Jack nodded, eating his chicken.

Sean found Lex right where Jack had said he'd be—at a small bar on Mills Lane at Cross

Way. Cross Way was exactly what its name said: a large junction where every transportation vehicle operating between uptown and downtown met. Mills Lane was a small lane of bars and food shops a few minutes off the junction.

Lex sat at the bar, hunched over his rum glass. He was far too thin a man with pasty, sagging dark skin, a sign of too much alcohol abuse over the years. Lex looked up at him with blood-red eyes and smiled, revealing a missing front tooth. While Lex was a 24/7 drunk, he was reliable. The bar was dark, with a few scattered patrons. The barmaid, a plump Indian woman, smiled at him as he walked up to the bar. He noted her left lazy eye.

"Wha' yu' drinkin'?" she asked, with gold-capped front teeth.

"Coke, clean," he told her and pulled up a seat beside Lex. She looked him over good before moving to get him his Coke. After she had served him, Sean turned his full attention to Lex.

"How yu' doin'?" Sean asked him.

"Bad, real bad. Lost my job."

"Again?" Sean asked, disappointed. Lex had started the job, which he had found for him, a month ago. Come to think if it, he was always finding Lex jobs. He didn't mind because Lex was a good informer. Because he was always drunk or pretended to be, he was overlooked by just about everyone.

Lex finished his drink and waved the

barmaid over. "Same," he told her and she poured Lex some Ray and Nephew, Jamaican white run, straight. How he drank the rum straight was beyond Sean. That type of rum was so strong it was like gasoline.

"So, wha' do yu' have?"

"Mike's in Cayman," Lex told him. "He's workin' on some'ting big," Lex said under his breath.

"How big?" Sean wanted to know.

"Major shipment comin' in a couple of months." Lex nodded, taking a sip of his rum. The man didn't even react to the intensity of the liquor.

"Which end?"

"Don't know," Lex said with a slur.

"That's it?" Sean asked, disappointed.

"I hear he wants yu' dead," Lex whispered.

"Tell me some'ting I don't know." Sean couldn't help being agitated. He had hoped to get more out of Lex. Knowing about the shipment was good, but he wanted details. He couldn't exactly do a bust when he didn't know where the drugs would be.

"I suggest yu' watch yu' back." Lex gave him a warning look. "I hear he's payin'."

Sean's guard went up.

"Yu' been watched," Lex whispered.

Instantly Sean took note of everyone in the place. He didn't see anyone out of the ordinary. No one was even looking at them. The bar-maid was busy drying glasses.

"Thanks for the heads-up," Sean said and pulled out a hundred dollar bill and placed it in front of Lex on the bar. Sean got up and left without touching his drink. All he could think on was Kelee. He had taken her out tonight; any- and everyone in the club had seen them together. He really didn't want Kelee in harm's way, but he also couldn't stay away from her either. The timing was really bad. He had to take care of Mike.

Sean heard laughter when he entered his apartment. Kelee and Jack were seated at the kitchen table playing dominoes.

"Who's winnin'?" He walked over to them. From what he was seeing Kelee was winning. He also knew Jack was letting her win. He was a killer when it came to dominoes. In all the years Sean knew Jack he had only won three games against him.

"Hi." Kelee flashed him a smile that made him pause. God, she was beautiful. Jack grinned at him and he went to the refrigerator and got himself a beer. He leaned against the counter watching them finish their game. Kelee won of course and was real happy about it. Jack pretended at be disappointed for a brief moment.

"I'm gonna' say good night," Jack said, getting up. "It was nice meetin' yu', Kelee." He smiled at her.

"Yu' too, an' thanks for letting me beat yu',"

Kelee said with a huge smile. Jack looked at Sean and laughed when he shrugged.

"Yu' welcome; hope to see yu,' again," Jack told her and headed for the front door.

"I'll be right back," Sean said to Kelee and followed Jack out.

"Wha' did he have?" Jack asked as they headed towards the elevators.

"Big shipment, no location, and Mike has paid eyes on me," Sean said.

"Not good." Jack looked at him, worried. "If he's watchin,' wha' 'bout Kelee?"

"I'll jus' have to keep her close," he said with a smile.

"Knew yu' would." Jack pressed the down button. "I like her," Jack told him, getting on the elevator. "Later," he said as the doors started to close.

"Later," Sean told him and headed back down the hall to Kelee.

Kelee had just finished packing away the dominoes in their box when Sean reentered the apartment. She looked at him, glad he was back. Jack had been great company, but she wanted to be with Sean. The look in his eyes said he wanted the same thing. This was it. No turning back; she wanted him too much.

"Missed me?" he asked with a sexy smirk, which made her smile. She looked up into his stunning eyes and felt that familiar rush. Her breath got caught in her throat and she had to take a deep breath to steady the flutter in her heart. He pulled her into his arms, and his mouth devoured hers in a hungry kiss that promised nothing but pure pleasure. She wrapped her arms around his neck. His hands found her behind and bought her closer to him. She felt his sex harden against her belly. She moaned and pressed into him. She opened her mouth, welcoming the sweet invasion of his tongue.

Sean lifted her and took her into the bedroom. Kelee noticed the large king-size bed with its matching chests. He placed her on her feet at the foot of the bed. His eyes were filled with extreme desire. She reached down, pulling at his shirt. He pulled his shirt over his head, revealing a smooth muscular chest, with six-pack abs. He was magnificent. Kelee ran her hand down his chest and over his stomach. She noticed his holster and that he wore his gun behind his back. He undid his holster and placed it with his .45 on the end table. Without missing a beat he pulled her back into his arms, devouring her lips in a scorching kiss. Kelee melted into him. He released her mouth and stepped back, looking at her. She slowly took off her shirt and bra under his watchful eyes. Her nipples hardened as his eyes fell to her breasts. He moistened his lips as she undid her jeans and pulled them off. She stood before him in her panties, felt beautiful under his roving eyes that were filled with desire for her. She loved the way he looked at her. It spoke of his desire for her. The same desire also consumed her every being, a desire that only he could fulfill. His eyes met hers, and he smiled, moving towards her. He knelt before her and reached for her panties, pulling them down. She rested her hands on his shoulders as she stepped out of her underwear. He pressed his warm lips into her navel, setting off fireworks throughout her body. He stood up and removed his pants; she watched with anticipation as he revealed himself to her. He stood before her, proud and fully aroused. She suppressed a moan at the sight of him. She couldn't wait to feel him. He pulled her into his arms, kissing her until she was weak. She loved the way he kissed her. It was like he wanted to consume her. He guided her onto the bed, never breaking their kiss. His mouth moved down, consuming her breasts as his hand found her sex. Her legs flowed open, welcoming the invasion of his very skilled fingers. She moaned his name, digging her fingers into his shoulders as he caressed her until she was a writhing mess. He reached into the nightstand for a condom; she was grateful he had thought of them this time. She had bought some but they were at Lori's; she hadn't planned on making love with him tonight. But he was prepared and she was ready. She watched him as he put the protection on. She gazed into his eyes as he came over her; she welcomed him, sighing as he pressed into her, filling both her body and her soul.

Kelee clung to Sean moaning his name. She moved with him as he caressed her in the most intimate of ways. She reveled in the strength of him inside her. He cradled her as he moved against her, looking deeply into her eyes. Kelee felt an incredible freedom with him. His movements quickened, she met his every move, crying out his name as her body exploded with pleasure. She felt him stiffen a few seconds later, as he moaned her name. For what seemed like an eternity, neither of them moved. The only sounds in the room were their heavy breathing and heartbeats coming back to normal.

Sean pulled Kelee into his arms, cradling her against him. She ran her hands over his smooth muscular chest. They lay there in silence for a while, just holding each other. Making love with him was even better than she had imagined. Once again, Kelee couldn't shake the feeling of knowing Sean. It was crazy, because she didn't. She looked into his face. He gave her a sweet smile.

"Wha' wrong?" he asked softly.

"I don't want to scare yu'," she began, and paused.

"Tell me," he urged.

"I keep getting the strangest feeling that I know yu'," she said and felt his body stiffen.

She had scared him. She sat up, looking at him, worried. She wished she had kept her mouth shut. "I know we've never met before, but I can't shake the feeling that I know yu'. I know it must sound crazy to yu', but yu' are so familiar to me."

"That's a good 'ting," he said and pulled her down on top of him, kissing her deeply. She breathed a sigh of relief, glad that she hadn't scared him. She liked him and she really didn't want to scare him off.

Sean had a meeting with Jack and the police commissioner. He didn't want to take Kelee home, but the meeting was important. He dropped her off at Lori's an hour later, promising to call her. She gave him a lingering kiss before letting him go. He didn't want to leave her, but he had to. As he drove back downtown, he felt really guilty for lying to her. Her telling him how familiar he was to her after they had made love had only served to fuel his guilt. In a few days they'd be at View Cost where it all had started. He'd tell her there. He had to; he really couldn't lie to her anymore—not after last night. Making love to her was even better than he had remembered. The chemistry between them was overwhelming. He couldn't stop thinking about her and all the things he wanted to share with her while she was in St. Pala. He wondered how long she'd stay after her niece was born. He had to get her to stay longer. Maybe when he revealed who he was to her at View Coast she would extend her stay in St. Pala.

Chapter 8

Kelee was on cloud nine, a place she hadn't been before. And it was all because of Sean St. John. He was absolutely perfect and wonderful and she couldn't wait to see him again. He had told her she might not see him until the weekend in View Coast, because of a case he was working on. She didn't mind, not after last night. Last night had left a lasting and pleasurable impression on her. The weekend was only a few days away, and she couldn't wait to be with him again. Of course Lori noticed the change in her right away, as she joined her for a late breakfast.

"Someone had a good night." She grinned with curiosity.

Kelee sipped her coffee, grinning. "No comment," she said.

"Oh, yu' goin' to comment." Lori glared at her.

"He took me to a friend's birthday party at the

Swan, then we ended up at his apartment and I'm not giving yu' any details, married woman," Kelee told her sternly.

"As long as yu' had a good time." Lori gave her a curious look.

"Yu' see the look on my face?" Kelee said with a huge smile.

"I see it." Lori laughed. "So, when yu' seein' him again?"

"This weekend at View Coast; he's working some big case," Kelee told her

"Yeah, the Curve case."

"What's the Curve case?" she asked.

"Curve's a local businessman and drug dealer. Sean's been trying to put him away for a while now."

Now she understood why he kept running off. While he'd never talked about his work, Kelee got the feeling that he was very involved and serious about it.

"He doesn't talk 'bout it?" Lori asked her.

"Guess he didn't want to bother me with his work." She shrugged.

"That's Sean for yu'," Lori said. "He does have that air of mystery about him."

"Guess that has to do with his line of work." Kelee reached for a breakfast roll. She had to admit that she really didn't know that much about what Sean did on a daily basis. The fact was that she didn't want to take their relationship beyond them enjoying each other's company.

She would not be here that long to get attached to him. She recalled the connection she felt towards him, after they had made love. It bothered her, and she didn't know why.

"Wha' wrong?" Lori asked, concerned.

"Remember that feeling of familiarity I told yu' I had about Sean?"

"Yeah," Lori said and waited for her to continue.

"It's like I know him, or I should, but I know I don't. Last night was crazy and disturbing to the point that I had to tell him."

"How did he take it?"

"He thought it was a good thing."

"So what's the problem?"

"It scares me, the connection is so intense," she admitted.

"Are yu' scared yu' fallin' for him?" Lori asked. Her question stunned Kelee; she hadn't thought of that. There was no way she was falling for a man she hardly knew or had just met. That was straight up crazy.

"No, that's not it," Kelee told her with certainty. "I do like him, but not like that."

"Yu' sure?" Lori asked.

Kelee looked at her sister, wondering if she was right. No way. No way was she falling for Sean. That, she couldn't allow. She liked him, and she liked the sex, that was it. That was all there would ever be between them.

"I'm very sure," Kelee said sternly. As long as she believed it she'd be fine.

"So, relax and enjoy yu' time with him," Lori advised. Kelee agreed she would.

Chapter 9

View Coast was a tourist paradise. It was a
five-mile stretch of white sand beach with three
of the best resorts in St. Pala. There was another three miles of private homes and cabins
on the beach. They were staying at the Dawn
Resort, which was hosting the Appleton Rum
Festival. The place was buzzing with activity as
the staff set up the first party that night.

Kelee's room was next to Lori and Allan's on
the fourth floor. From her room Kelee could see
the beach and the massive pool below. A stage
was set up on the beach and sound checks were
being done. According to the itinerary, a
number of local artists were performing tonight.
Tomorrow they had a few American well-known
hip-hop artists along with locals on the list.

Kelee dressed in hip hugger jeans and a silver
satin tank. Then she went to check on Lori,
only to find her fussing with Allan over her not
liking anything she had bought to wear. Allan

was trying his best, but Kelee could see the frustration in his face.

"Why don't yu' go secure us a table? I'll finish up here," Kelee told him. Allan gave her a thankful look and left in a hurry.

Kelee gave Lori a scolding look.

Lori rolled her eyes at her and said, "Don't yu' start with me. It's his fault."

"Stop bitchin'," Kelee told her.

"I am not bitchin'!" Lori pouted.

"If yu' say so." Kelee picked up the sexy maternity tank with its flared end. She moved to help Lori put it on.

"Thanks," Lori mumbled. Kelee kissed her cheek, smiling at her. Lori smiled.

"Yu' think Sean's goin' to be here?" Kelee asked. She hadn't heard from him since yesterday and he'd promised he'd call before they left the house. He hadn't. She longed to see him, even though it had only been a few days since they'd parted. They had spent at least an hour talking on the phone last night, but it just wasn't enough; she wanted to see him.

"Don't worry, he'll be here," Lori reassured her.

They joined Allan in the grand ballroom where a fashion show was in progress. Kelee scanned the room; no Sean. To combat her anxiety Kelee focused on the show of local designers. The clothes were excellent. There was a lot more talent in St. Pala than she realized.

She enjoyed the fashion show. Afterwards they were informed that the buffet and bar were open by the pool. The buffet offered a wide variety of local and gourmet foods. The live show was scheduled to start an hour later.

Kelee was working on her second plate and still there was no sign of Sean, so she decided not to think of him and enjoyed what the festival had to offer. Allan got them a VIP spot, with lawn chairs. The first band was called Suns. They were a reggae band that played mostly classic reggae tunes. The band was in the middle of their second song when she sensed him. She didn't know how, but she did. She gazed over her shoulder to see him making his way over to them. He smiled at her and her heart skipped a beat. He was dressed in loose khaki slacks and a white T-shirt. His eyes remained fixed on her as he came to a stop at her side.

"Hey," he said, crouching down, looking at her.

"Hi." She smiled. She was happy to see him and she couldn't hide it.

"Lori, Allan," he said, gazing at them briefly.

"'Bout time yu' showed up," Lori told him and Kelee glared at her in disbelief.

"Forgive me?" Sean asked, looking at Kelee. She smiled and told him, "Forgiven."

"Care to join me?" Sean asked with a smile that made her jump out of her chair. She was ready to go with him.

"Don't stay out too late," Lori teased.

"Yes, Mother," Kelee threw back and heard them laugh.

Taking a hold of her hand, Sean led her away from the party and down the beach. The minute they were clear of the crowd that had gathered on the beach for the show, he pulled her into his arms, kissing her. She sighed and wrapped her arms around his neck, returning his kiss. His mouth gently possessed hers with an urgency that spoke of his passion for her. It made her heart sing; it also felt wonderful to be in his arms again.

"Miss me?" he asked, gently breaking their kiss.

"I thought yu' weren't coming," she said, caressing his stubbly cheek.

"An' leave yu' here alone, yu' mad?" he teased. She smiled.

"So why are yu' late?"

"Work."

"I'm glad yu' here," she told him, pulling his head down to hers. This time she kissed him as if she wanted to possess him. She heard him moan and it pleased her.

"Let's go to yu' room," he whispered in her ear.

"Do yu' have protection?" she asked and he grinned, pulling a condom from his pocket. They left the beach and headed up to her room. Once inside they were all over each other. They kissed and stumbled across the room as they undressed each other. Sean lifted her and took her into the bedroom, where they fell onto the bed in a heated kiss. Sean's lips left a trail of hot, moist kisses down her body, turning her into a quivering mess. She reached for him, pulling him over her, kissing him deeply. He pulled back, put the condom on and drove hard and fast into her. She wrapped her arms and legs around him, moaning his name as he moved against her. She bit into his shoulder as her body tightened with pleasure and burst into the ultimate release.

Kelee lay in Sean's arms, running her hand over his sleek chest muscles. She loved his body and the pleasure he gave her; she wished she could have him forever.

"Let's go for a walk," he suggested. She looked into his face.

"We could just stay here." She smiled, kissing his nipple.

"There's some'ting I want to show yu'." He ran his fingers through her hair, pulling her towards him, kissing her lightly.

"OK." She smiled, caressing his lips with her tongue.

Fifteen minutes later they walked down the beach, stopping here and there, kissing and playing like kids.

Tyce watched Sean and Kelee. They were locked in a lovers' embrace on the beach. He had been watching Kelee since she arrived at the hotel with her sister and her brother-in-law. For a moment he didn't think Sean would show, but to Tyce's disappointment, he had. Minutes before Sean had arrived he even contemplated approaching Kelee. He was glad he hadn't, because Sean would have seen him, which he didn't want. He watched them kiss. They really couldn't get enough of each other, which was a good thing. He could see just how much Sean was into Kelee; it would work to his advantage. He watched them as they strolled down the beach. The closer those two got the better. He walked away, returning to the concert to enjoy the rest of the show.

"There's some'ting I need to show yu," Sean told Kelee as they passed a private cottage on the beach. The part of the beach they were strolling was lined with small cottages, some owned by the hotel, some private.

"What is it?" she asked, excited.

"Yu'll see," he told her, gazing down at her. They continued down the beach. The cottages brought back memories of a wild summer Kelee had spent on this same beach. Most of it was a blur still. At that time she had smoked way too much marijuana and was too high half the time. But that was her past, one she wasn't all too proud of.

Sean started to lead her towards a cottage that was very familiar. It was still painted that cool blue color and the coconut tree was still there to the left of the house, hanging over it like an umbrella. Nothing about it had changed. She paused and Sean turned to look at her.

"Wha' is it?" he asked.

She'd been here before when she was younger. This was where she'd lost her virginity. She wanted to be with Sean, but not here. She wanted to tell him not here, but then he'd want to know why, and that, she couldn't tell him.

"Come on, it's all set up for us," he said in a too-cool voice. Kelee swallowed her past and smiled at him. He held a hand out to her and she placed her hand in his. He led her towards the cabin. At the door he pulled out a key and opened the door. Kelee hesitated. It didn't feel right. It felt strange. Sean pulled her inside, switching on the lights.

"Don't worry, yu' gonna' love it," he said. Kelee stood in the small living room, looking around the cottage. It was exactly how she had remembered it, cozy and welcoming. The furniture, she noted, was different; more modern pieces now accented the room. She could see that the kitchen/dining area had been remodeled. A flood of memories came rushing back at her. She felt uncomfortable; she couldn't stay here.

"Don't tell me yu' don't remember?" Sean

whispered in her ear. A cold shiver raced down Kelee's entire body. She jumped away from him. How did he know? He couldn't know. She looked into his eyes, noticed the wicked grin on his face. And for the first time she could place his eyes, his mouth . . . it was Mark.

"Oh, my God!" she exclaimed and covered her mouth, shocked. He knew exactly who she was.

"Mark?" she whispered. He nodded. It couldn't be. The Mark she knew back then had dreads and a full beard. No wonder she didn't recognize him. Suddenly her anger took over. He knew who she was and had played her for a fool.

"Sean Mark St. John," he said with a slight smile. He thought it was funny, playing with her the way he had. He knew they had been together, right here. She felt sick to her stomach. He had made love to her knowing who she was.

"Yu' son of a bitch!" she screamed. "Yu' knew an' yu' didn't say anything?"

She felt used and stupid. She had made love to him, told him how familiar he felt to her. He must have been laughing at her when she said it. Humiliation filled her, making her boiling mad. She recalled the look in his eyes then; now she knew why. He'd played with her in the worst way possible. The thought of them just making love only served to infuriate her even more.

"Come on, Kelee, yu' can't be mad at me.

Yu' have to admit it's funny. I mean, we spent five nights here together, how could yu' not remember me?" he asked, amused. He really thought it was funny.

"Go to hell!" she screamed and ran out of the cottage. She heard him calling after her as she ran all the way back to the hotel. She got to her room, locking the door behind her. Her heart was pounding hard against her chest. And then the tears started to roll down her cheeks. She threw herself across her bed and cried. A few minutes later she heard a knocking and Sean asking her to open the door. She didn't answer. She hated him for what he'd done to her.

Sean had made a big mistake, he realized as he walked away from Kelee's door. He just didn't think she'd react the way she had to his revealing who he was. He recalled the hurt in her eyes and it tore at him. He had played it all wrong. He should have told her. His cell phone rang. It was Jack.

"We found Adams." By Jack's tone, Sean knew it wasn't good.

"Is he alive?"

"Barely," Jack informed him. Sean breathed a sigh of relief. At least he was alive. Adams was tough; he knew he'd survive.

"Where is he?"

"Kings Hospital. Sean, he doesn't look too good," Jack said desolately.

"I'll be there in an hour," Sean told him and ended the call. He headed back to the beach where the concert was in full swing. He made his way to where Allan and Lori were. Lori looked up at him, concerned when she didn't see Kelee with him.

"Where's Kelee?" Lori asked, worried.

"She's in her room," Sean told her, feeling guilty about what he had done. Lori looked at him, concerned.

"What happened?"

"I have to go," he said. Lori looked at him.

"Some'ting wrong?" Allan asked.

"They found one of my men an' he doesn't look good."

Allan nodded at him, understanding.

"Tell Kelee I'm sorry an' I'll call her," he told Lori and left.

Kelee heard Lori calling her name. She dragged herself out of bed and went to the door. She had a headache from crying. She opened the door and Lori gasped when she saw her. Kelee knew she looked a mess from crying.

"What happened?" Lori asked, moving into the room and closing the door behind her. Kelee walked over to the sofa and dropped into the plush cushions. Lori sat beside her.

"What happened with yu' an' Sean?" Lori asked.

"He can go to hell!" she said, and she meant it.

"What happened?" Lori insisted.

Kelee took a deep breath and told her everything. When she was done, Lori stared at her, stunned.

"I can't believe he'd do that to yu'," Lori exclaimed.

"And the worst part is that he thought it was funny that I didn't recognize him."

"Well, that part is kinda' funny." Lori grinned.

"Now yu' taking his side," Kelee fumed.

"No, no, what he did was wrong, but yu' not recognizin' him is funny." Lori giggled and Kelee frowned at her. "He did tell me to tell yu' that he was sorry."

"Like that's supposed to make it better. I hate him for humiliating me the way he did. As long as I'm here I don't want to hear his name or see him. Yu' can tell him that, and I mean it," Kelee told her sternly.

"Yu' sure?" Lori asked with uncertainty.

"Yes," she said firmly. She had made up her mind. She was done with Sean.

Lori looked at her, disappointed. "I don't think he meant to hurt yu', Kelee," Lori started. Kelee glared at her.

"I told yu' I don't want to hear any'ting about him!" Kelee snapped.

"OK." Lori shrugged. "I'm going to bed." Lori left her alone with her tormented thoughts.

Sean felt like crap as he drove back to the city. Kelee hated him and it was his fault. He should have been honest with her from the start; instead, he had played with her emotions. He recalled the disgust and hate in her eyes tonight and it bothered him. His little revenge game and backfired in the worst way. She hated him. He didn't want her hating him. This wasn't the way he wanted things between them. The minute he saw to Adams he'd return to View Coast to see her. She had to accept his apology; he had to make her understand that he never meant to hurt her. He prayed she'd listen to him.

Chapter 10

Sean got to the hospital to find Adams awake and talking. He was battered and badly bruised, but he was alive, thank God. Adams's wife Carla was by his side. Sean could see the relief in her eyes as she looked at him. Jack was there also.

"How yu' feelin'?" Sean asked, moving to Adams's bedside. Adams tried to give him a smile, but it was a difficult task for him.

"Glad to be here," he managed to say.

"Whoever did this to yu' will pay," Sean promised. "Where's Penn?" he asked.

"Don't know; they took us by surprise. I was blindfolded, didn't even know where I was," Adams said with difficulty. "I think Penn was taken somewhere else." He coughed. Sean laid a comforting hand on his shoulder.

"We'll find him," Sean promised. Adams gave him a confident look. "Get some rest," Sean told him.

"Yu' need to find who did this to him," Carla

insisted. He could see the anger in her eyes. He understood her pain. Both Adams and Penn ▮▮▮his friends. It hurt him to see Adams look-▮▮▮▮▮he did. It bothered him even more ▮▮▮▮where Penn was or if he was suffer-▮▮▮te as Adams. He felt hopeless, but ▮▮▮▮▮t show it. He had people depending on him.

"I promise I will," he told Carla with determination. She nodded, satisfied with his promise. He meant to keep that promise.

Jack followed him outside to the parking lot. "Where did yu' find him?" Sean asked.

"He was dumped in front of the office. The car had no plates and it was completely tinted, security didn't see any'ting."

Sean sighed in frustration. "Where's Kurt right now?" If Sean could get his hands on Mike's brother Kurt, maybe he could get something out of him.

"Last I heard he was in Jamaica," Jack said.

"I want him taken in for questionin' the minute he's back here," Sean told Jack. "I want a man on Adams."

"I called Ian; he's on his way."

Ian was an undercover cop who did a lot of security detail for them.

"Lex came by the office earlier lookin' for yu.' He wouldn't tell me any'ting, only that it was important."

"He probably has some'ting on Mike," Sean speculated.

"Or he needs another drink," Jack said.

Sean knew Jack was probably right. But Lex was a good source and if he came to see him, he'd like to know why. For some reason Jack intimidated Lex, no matter how kind Jack was to him. Lex just wouldn't talk to Jack.

"Did he say where he'd be?"

"His usual spot." Jack shrugged.

If Lex had something, he needed to talk to him now. After seeing what they had done to Adams, he needed something, anything. He had to find Penn. Suddenly Sean had a feeling that Lex knew something about where he was.

"Call me if any'ting comes up," Sean said, heading for his jeep.

"Yu' headin' back to View Coast?" Jack asked. Sean paused and thought of what had previously gone down between him and Kelee. He really wanted to go back to her, but he couldn't; he had to see Lex tonight. He'd see Kelee when she came back to the city.

"No, I'll be in the city," Sean told Jack and got into his jeep.

Sean must have gone to almost every bar in Cross Way; no one knew where Lex was. Sean even checked Lex's mother's house, but she hadn't seen Lex in a couple of days. He had always been able to find Lex. Something didn't feel right. Sean was starting to get worried.

Chapter 11

Kelee woke the next morning with a hangover; she had consumed almost half a bottle of wine last night after Lori had left. She had needed to get drunk last night, so she wouldn't think of Sean and how he had humiliated her. Her head was pounding and she needed caffeine. She showered, dressed and headed downstairs for breakfast. A nice spread was set up in the dining room. It was almost eleven and the dining room was pretty empty. She got her coffee and a large bowl of fruit salad and a muffin. She was pouring herself a second cup when she saw Tyce enter the dining room. Their eyes met and he smiled at her; she smiled back. He made his way over to her. He was dressed in jeans and a white polo shirt with his sunglasses hanging from the front.

"I thought I might see yu' here," he said.

"Yu' were looking for me?" she said, surprised

that he would be. She hadn't told him she'd be here.

"Just 'bout everyone comes to this festival," he said, pouring some juice. "Can I join yu'?" he asked with a charming smile.

"Sure," she told him and headed to the table where she was sitting. He sat across from her.

"Yu' been enjoyin' the festival so far?" he asked, his eyes focused on her.

"Yes, it's been great so far." She mustered up the best smile she could as memories of last night came flooding back at her. She had made up her mind last night to put Sean behind her and enjoy the rest of her stay in St. Pala. She would not let him ruin her stay here.

"Yu' here with someone?" he asked tentatively.

"No," she said and watched as his brows arched with interest.

"Care to join me for the rest of the festivities?" he asked with a gentle smile.

"Love to," she said. Sean Mark St. John could go to hell.

Kelee spent the rest of the day going to different events in the surrounding area with Tyce. He was charming and funny and she enjoyed his company. Around five, Kelee went to her room to rest up for the night concert. She had promised to meet Tyce for dinner an hour before the concert. She was relaxing after a shower when Lori joined her in her room.

"I haven't seen yu' all day; don't tell me yu' been locked up in here?"

"Hell, no. I've been out with Tyce," Kelee told her with a smile.

"Tyce who?"

"Remember the guy who came to my rescue after I was robbed?"

"Oh. So I guess Sean is forgotten?"

"Who?" Kelee asked in a nasty sarcastic tone.

"OK. I see yu' moved on. Just don't move too fast," Lori warned.

"Tyce is good company, nothing more," Kelee said.

"Be careful," Lori warned.

"Yes, Mother," Kelee teased. Lori rolled her eyes.

For dinner, Tyce took Kelee to a small restaurant not far from the resort. He had told her that the food was better than the hotel's and he was right. Kelee enjoyed every bite of the jerk chicken pasta with cream sauce. Tyce had fish and pasta; the fish smelled and looked delicious. She sampled Tyce's dish; it was absolutely divine. They shared fried bananas and coconut ice cream for dessert. After dinner, they strolled back to the hotel. Tyce asked Kelee's suggestions on a house he wanted to decorate. Kelee shared with him some of her decorating secrets. They found Lori and Allan in the VIP section. Kelee introduced Tyce. Allan looked Tyce over briefly with curiosity. They all settled and enjoyed the concert.

Chapter 12

Sean was distracted with thoughts of Kelee. He had called the house a number of times and she had refused to take his calls. He decided to give her some time to calm down; it had been two days and all he could think of was Kelee. Work had kept him busy; he had planned on stopping by the house to see her, but he was busy trying to find Penn and Lex. He needed to see her. He needed to talk to her. He needed her and it was unnerving to him. Once again she had gotten to him. He had thought he was in control of the situation: he was wrong.

"Yu' OK?" Jack asked, walking into his office.

"Yeah."

Jack gave him a concerned look.

"Wha's goin' on?" Jack sat before him.

"No'ting." Sean sighed. "Wha' yu' got for me?"

"No one has seen Lex."

Sean sat back. "This is not good, I can feel it."

Sean knew Mike was responsible for Lex's

disappearance. Mike had been hiding out in Cayman for the last couple of months. He couldn't stay in Cayman forever, and the minute he came back to St. Pala he would be arrested. Sean intended to pay him back for what he did to Adams. And if Penn wasn't found alive, Sean had every intention of killing Mike. He had been building his case against Mike for years now. Mike would be arrested for everything from tax evasion to money laundering. Sean had linked him to a number of murders. There was nothing but jail time waiting for Mike, once he was back in St. Pala.

Kelee was doing her best not to think of Sean, which was difficult. He haunted her very dreams. She still wanted him and she hated it. She had refused to take any of his calls. She needed to distance herself from him. It was best.

"Why don't yu' just talk to him?" Lori asked. They were sitting on the veranda over breakfast.

"No," she said sternly.

"He's miserable. Yu' miserable, wha's the point?"

"He lied to me. That's the point!" Kelee injected feeling, her anger rising. He had made a fool of her. She couldn't forget that.

"I think he's tryin' to apologize an' yu' should listen to him."

"No."

"Damn, yu' can be hard-headed sometimes."
Lori shook her head, disappointed.

Nadine came out with the cordless phone.
"It's for yu'," she told Kelee, handing the phone
to her.

"Is it Sean?" she asked.

"No," Nadine said and Kelee took the phone.

"Hello?" she said into the phone.

"Hi," Tyce said.

"Hi," she greeted him back.

"I need yu' help," he said.

"With what?"

"I'm shoppin' for some furniture today, an' I
don't know wha' will go with wha'. Can yu' help
me? I'll pay yu'," he pleaded.

"Yu' don't have to, I'd love to help. Give me
something to do today," she told him and heard
him breathe a sigh of relief.

"Yu' drivin' or yu' want me to send a car for
yu'?" he asked.

"Where are yu' shopping?" she said.

"Cross Way Mall."

"I'll meet you there," she said. "I have some
shopping to do myself."

"Let's meet at the Kan's coffee shop," he suggested.

"Give me an hour," Kelee told him.

"Thank yu', thank yu," Tyce said, relieved.
Kelee ended the call to find Lori glaring at her.

"What?" she asked, knowing what was coming.
Lori didn't like Tyce and she had said it more

than once. Kelee really didn't care. Tyce was a nice man and he hadn't made a pass at her, which she appreciated. It also made it easier to be around him.

"Yu' know wha' yu' doin' is wrong?"

"I'm helping the man pick out furniture. What's wrong with that?"

"I know yu' mad at Sean, but this Tyce person is not the right way to go," Lori said.

"I don't want to hear anything about *him*," Kelee told her, got up and left to go change.

Sean knew something big was up when the prime minister called an emergency meeting with all the heads of security on St. Pala. He also had a gut feeling that Mike was the reason. He and Jack walked into the conference room and all eyes turned to them. Minus the prime minister, those present were Jaydan Banks, senior super-intendent of police, a big brown man who de-manded respect. Jan's second in command, su-perintendent Paul Thomas, sat beside him. Paul was the Indian version of Jan. The commissioner of police, Frank Tam, who was Chinese/black, was also present. This was big, Sean thought as he greeted them. They were all friends of his, with whom he had worked closely over the years. Sean got himself a cup of coffee and took a seat. Jack sat beside him.

He was about to ask if any of them knew what

the emergency meeting was about, when the prime minster, Henry Hamilton, walked in with his advisor Kris Oliver. Henry was a lean, middle-aged black man with silver hair. His advisor Kris was white/Indian with striking gray eyes.

"Thank you all for comin' at such short notice," Henry said as he sat at the head of the table. All eyes were on him. "I've been informed that there's a boat of cocaine comin' in a few days. I want that boat!"

Sean thought of Lex and what he had told him about a shipment coming in. There was no doubt in Sean's mind that Lex's disappearance had something to do with the shipment. Lex knew too much, and they had gotten to him.

"Wha's the point of entry?" Sean asked.

"That we don't know yet, but I want all points covered. Whatever reinforcement yu' need yu' got it," Henry told them.

Henry spent the next half hour briefing them on the situation and the importance of them stopping the drugs from coming into St. Pala.

After leaving the meeting Sean and Jack decided to have some lunch.

"Yu' 'tink Lex is in this, don't yu'?" Jack asked after they had ordered.

"Yeah," Sean said.

"'Tink Mike's people got to him?"

"If they haven't, he's hidin'."

The waitress came with their food and that was when he saw her, laughing and smiling, with another man in a coffee shop across the way. Jack looked in the direction he was looking. The man touched her arm. All Sean could see was another man touching Kelee. He felt rage come over him. Who the hell was he? What was she doing with him? Why was she letting him touch her? Sean watched them as they got up and left the café. The man had his hand on the small of her back.

Sean looked at Jack, who was still watching Kelee and the man.

"I thought yu' were together?" Jack said.

"Yu' know him?" Sean asked, heated. What the hell was she doing with him? She couldn't have moved on that quick. What the hell was wrong with her? It took all of his restraint to not walk over there and drag her away.

"He's a businessman."

"I want to know who he's affiliated with."

Jack look at him, concerned. "Yu' 'tink he's associated with Curve?"

"He could be," Sean said. "Lex said they were watchin' me."

"Maybe yu' should warn her," Jack insisted.

"She's upset with me right now."

"Yu' two had a fallin' out already? That's quick." Jack gave him an inquiring look.

"It's a long story." Sean sighed.

"I'm listenin'." Jack sat back, waiting for the

rest of the story. Sean gave him the short version of what had happened between them. Jack was laughing so hard Sean had to kick him under the table to get him to stop.

"Wait till Mavis hears this one."

"Yu' tell her an' yu' fired," Sean threatened.

"Yeah, right." Jack grinned. "Yu' really like Kelee, don't yu'?" Jack asked on a more serious note.

"I more than like her," Sean said. Jack sat back with a surprised expression. Sean really was in love with Kelee, had been since he first met her ten years ago. And the thought of her ending up in danger because of him was nerve wracking. He had to make sure she was protected at all cost.

Chapter 13

"Sean called," Lori told Kelee as she walked into the kitchen. Lori and Nadine were shelling pigeon peas at the small dining table. It was almost one in the afternoon. The sky was dark and rain was coming down hard. Lori and Kelee had planned to go shopping but the rain had changed their plans.

"Good for him," Kelee said, getting a glass of water from the refrigerator.

"He wants yu' to call him. He said it's important," Lori insisted.

"Good for him," Kelee repeated and joined them at the table.

"Yu' not goin' to call him?" Lori asked.

"No." Kelee started to help shelling the peas.

Suddenly the rain stopped and the sun came out. Flash periods of rains were a regular occurrence in the Caribbean.

"So are we still going shopping for the baby?" Kelee asked.

"Sure, why not?" Lori pushed away from the table.

"Yu' won't believe this," Jack said, entering his office. Sean was on the phone with another one of his informers, who didn't have much to give him. Mike's people were starting to cover their tracks. It was getting harder to find out anything about his operation. Sean told his informant to call him if he heard anything and gave Jack his attention.

"His name is Tyce Thomas and he's Mike's second cousin an' business partner."

An undeniable fear raced through Sean. All he could think of was Kelee. She had no idea what was going on and she was definitely in danger. He had to get to Kelee before something happened to her. Sean immediately got on the phone, only to be told by Nadine that Kelee and Lori had gone shopping. He immediately called Lori's cell but it went straight to voice mail. He left a message asking her to call him immediately. He had to get to Kelee before they did.

Kelee gazed over at Lori, who was fast asleep in the passenger seat, and smiled. The minute Lori had gotten into the car she had fallen asleep. They were heading home after hours of shopping for the baby. Kelee gazed at her sister's belly while she waited at a light, wondering if she'd ever be in that position. She couldn't see it on her, but it was beautiful on her sister. Kelee had just turned off the main road onto the sloping road that led up the hill when she saw the black jeep blocking her path. The hood was up. The road was narrow with only two lanes, so Kelee carefully inched her way to overtake the jeep. She could see the driver buried under the hood as she passed. She returned her attention to the road, and that was when she saw him. She hit her brakes. He was masked and he had an M-16 aimed right at her. Lori had come awake with the sudden stop of the car.

"Wha'?" Lori asked, looking at her. Kelee looked at her pregnant sister, frightened. Lori looked at the man with the gun aimed at them.

"Oh, God," Lori gasped. "Stay calm, do whatever he says."

Kelee looked at Lori. Silently she prayed he wouldn't hurt them, especially Lori's unborn child. Suddenly there was a tap on Lori's side of the car and they looked to see the man that was under the hood, with a gun pointed at Lori. He, too, was masked.

Kelee started to shake.

"Get out!" the man on Kelee's side screamed at her. Kelee looked at Lori. Lori quickly took her hand. "Now!" the man demanded. Kelee jumped and reached for the door handle as a tear rolled down her cheek. She looked at Lori, who also had tears in her eyes.

Kelee's heart was racing with fear as she stepped from the jeep. The man grabbed her and shoved her towards their jeep. Kelee screamed. The man grabbed her from behind and placed a cloth over her face. Kelee panicked, kicking and screaming. Her screams only came out as muffled noise. The scent of the cloth burnt her eyes and nose, and then everything went black.

Sean was about to leave his office when he got the call. They had found a man's body near a junkyard in the parish of Caldon, south of the capital of St. Pala. The thought of it being Penn or Lex had his stomach in knots. It took Sean five minutes to reach the junkyard. A part of the yard was filled with rusty crushed cars, the other part was a mechanic shop. A few cop cars were there. An officer he knew as Sam Manning was questioning the workers. Sam was the one who had called him. Sam was tall, thin, and dark with rough features.

"Do yu' know who he is?" Sean asked as Sam took him down a lane of cars.

"No," Sam told him. "It kinda' hard to tell, the way he is," he said.

The body was naked and face down in a puddle of blood. Sean had seen a few executions like this before. It was Mike's signature style. From the body type and coloring it wasn't Penn, but Sean knew it was Lex. On closer inspection Sean noted the five bullet holes in the back of Lex's head. The number of holes in his head told Sean that Lex's face was completely gone. Lex knew too much and now he was dead. Sean thought of his missing man, Penn, as he stared at Lex's body. He feared he'd find Penn the same way. There was a reason why Adams was let go. It was a warning. Sean had to be extremely careful.

"Yu' know who he is?" Sam asked.

Sean looked at him. "Yeah, he was one of my best informants." He walked away. He had to get to Kelee.

Kelee felt like she was floating. Slowly she opened her eyes and looked around. She wasn't in her room. Where was she? Then it hit her. She had been kidnapped. Fear gripped her, causing her heart to race. Who would want to kidnap her? This was crazy. She barely knew anyone in St. Pala. Swallowing her fear, she sat up in the four-poster bed she was on. The room was large and barely decorated. Besides the bed it held a long double-drawer chest and an armchair. She noted the window with its curtains drawn, which made the room dark. She got up and went to the door; cautiously she reached for the knob. Her hand shook as she gripped the handle. She slowly turned the handle. It was locked. She slammed her hand against the door, rattling the knob.

"Let me out!" she screamed at the top of her lungs. But no one came. She banged on the door for a good ten minutes, but still no one responded. Defeated, Kelee walked over to the window, pulled the curtains back and opened the window. She saw nothing but dense trees and a gravel yard below. She was too far up to even try going out the window. There was no way out for her, her kidnapper had seen to that. Closing the window, Kelee looked around the room. She searched the chest but found it empty. Frustrated, she returned to the bed where she curled up and cried herself to sleep.

Quietly he sat on the side of the bed looking down at Kelee as she slept. She was so beautiful. Her face was stained with tears. She had been crying, obviously scared from being kidnapped. He brushed back a strand of hair off her cheek and she moaned, coming awake. He smiled at her. She sprang up, throwing her arms around his neck.

"Oh, Sean, thank God yu' found me," she cried. He wrapped his arms around her, inhaling her distinct perfume scent. "Please take me home," she begged.

He knew she was going to hate him, but he had to keep her safe and this was the only way.

"I can't," he told her and felt her stiffen. She pulled away from him, looking into his face. He watched as she realized the situation.

"Yu' did this. Why?" she asked, confused.

"I need yu' to stay here for a while."

Her eyes flared with anger. "Are yu' crazy? Yu' can't keep me here."

Sean understood her anger, but he had to keep her safe. "The kitchen is fully stocked and Kris will be keeping an eye on yu'."

"Kris?" she asked, confused.

"He's here to protect yu'," he told her.

"Protect me from what?"

"I really don't have time to explain every'ting right now. I just came by to make sure that yu' OK." He got up and started for the door.

"Yu' can't leave me here!" Kelee cried, running after him. She grabbed him at the door. He turned to look down at her. Her eyes were filled with tears. He hated doing this to her, but her safety was of utmost importance.

"I'll be back soon," he promised and saw anger flare in her eyes again.

"Yu' can't do this! This is crazy!"

"I need yu' to stay here."

"No!" she screamed, brushing at the tears that rolled down her cheeks.

"I'm not goin' to lock yu' in. But if yu' give Kris any trouble he will lock yu' in here."

"Please don't do this," she pleaded, and it tugged at his heart. He had no choice. He had to protect her. He pulled out a cell phone and handed it to her.

"Yu' can call Lori. She knows yu' safe," he told her. She took the phone. He walked away.

Kelee couldn't believe that Sean had just walked away the way he did. She didn't know how long she stood there with her mouth gaping open. Sean had kidnapped her and on top of that he refused to give her an explanation. She left her room to find herself at the top of a hallway. She walked to the end of the hall to the stairs. The house was barely furnished, she noted as she entered the living room. It only had a large sectional sofa and a large TV. A very large intimidating man was watching the TV. The evening news was on. Kelee instantly noted his gun beside him on the sofa. He looked at her, not moving.

"Hi, yu' must be Kris," she said to him and he gave her a slight smile and nodded.

"Which way is the kitchen?" she asked. She was starting to get hungry. He pointed to his left. She went that way; in the kitchen she found bags of groceries sitting on the counter. She started to unpack the food. She was glad when she saw the jar of pasta sauce and bow tie pasta. She made a quick pasta meal.

She poked her head out of the kitchen door and asked Kris if he'd like some pasta.

He smiled at her, surprised, and said, "Thanks."

She took him a bowl of pasta and joined him on the sofa to watch the news.

"So how long have yu' worked for Sean?" she asked and Kris looked at her, contemplating his answer. She waited for him to answer.

"Three years," Kris finally told her after shoveling a forkful of pasta into his mouth. She could tell he was a man who liked his food. She wondered how many meals she'd have to make to convince him to let her go. Her culinary skills weren't that good, but from the way he was enjoying the pasta, she knew she had him on that dish.

"What exactly do yu' do for him?"

"Security mostly."

"Yu' mean baby-sitting," she taunted and he smiled. At least he had a sense of humor.

"Yu' could call it that." He stuffed more pasta into his mouth.

"Do yu' know why he's keeping me here?"

"He said yu' needed protection," Kris said.

"From who?" She was curious. She wanted to know why Sean would go to such an extreme to protect her, and who the hell was he protecting her from?

"Don't know. Yu' have to ask him."

Kelee didn't exactly like Kris's answer, but

she doubted she'd get any information out of him. She finished her pasta.

After she washed the dishes Kelee returned to her room. She noticed an overnight bag at the foot of the bed. She opened it to find toiletries and some of her clothes inside. Sean had gone to the house and gotten her clothes. She wondered how long he'd planned her abduction. The thought of it all only made her steaming mad.

She called Lori.

"Are yu' OK?" Lori asked upon hearing her voice.

"Yeah, I'm fine." She frowned. "Do yu' have any idea why I'm here?"

"I think it might have to do with a case he's workin' on," Lori said.

"What case?"

"It has to do with a drug dealer named Curve."

Kelee recalled Lori telling her about some big case Sean was working on involving a businessman and drug dealer.

"And what the hell does that have to do with me?"

"He feels the need to protect yu'."

"This is a bit drastic, don't yu' think?"

"I know, Kelee, but just hang in there. I know Sean and if he 'tinks this is best, it is."

"Thanks for taking his side." Kelee rolled her eyes.

"I'm not, but I know him an' I trust him."

"Good for yu'. All it's gotten me is locked up

in some strange house with a baby-sitter who happens to have a gun."

"Yu' safe, don't worry," Lori reassured her.

"Anyway, how are yu'?"

"Good. The baby's kickin' like crazy; I hardly slept last night."

"This isn't exactly how I want to spend my vacation, locked away from yu'."

"I know," Lori said, disappointed.

They talked for the next half hour before saying good night.

Kelee took a shower and changed into a sleeping shirt and went to bed. She was about to fall asleep when the phone rang. It was Sean.

"Yu' OK?" he asked.

"Yeah, if I was home and not here," she snapped.

"Yu'll be home soon, I promise," he said in a gently soothing tone. "It's late, get some sleep. We'll talk soon."

"Sean?" she started but the call ended.

Chapter 14

"Kelee OK?" Jack asked.

"She's upset," Sean said. Jack laughed and shook his head.

"Kidnappin' her was a bit extreme," Jack said.

"I know," he said. "She wouldn't talk to me when I tried to call her an' I didn't have time to explain 'tings to her."

They were watching the loading docks from the jeep parked in the shadows. They had gotten a tip that the boat was coming in at this dock tonight. While this was the designated dock, Sean wasn't about to leave the other docks uncovered. He wasn't taking any chances. Besides Jack he had ten other undercover cops in various locations with him. Six covered the docks with him and Jack and the other four were just off the main road that led away from the docks. He also had the coast guard on standby, with others to take the boat if it tried to leave the docks.

An hour went by as Sean and Jack watched the

dock through night vision binoculars. It was almost three A.M. and nothing. Sean called the other four locations that were under surveillance. They reported nothing.

"'Tink they know we here?" Jack said, rubbing his temples.

"Maybe, maybe not." Sean rotated his neck. He was getting tired and that was when he heard it. It was the low hum of an engine. Jack heard it, too. They looked at each other. Sean informed the others, then he and Jack got out of the jeep, guns drawn.

From a safe spot they watched as a small luxury yacht docked. Moments later Kurt emerged with six heavily armed men. Kurt looked around the dock. Sean had instructed the men not to do anything until Kurt and the drugs were off the boat. They watched as two men emerged with an oversize tub. Just then a large black van came roaring onto the dock. The van came to a stop and a man jumped out. Sean didn't recognize the driver. He told his men to lie back. He wanted the drugs off the boat before he made a move. He watched as Kurt stepped off the boat and greeted the man. The men doing the unloading placed the tub on the dock, then went back down only to emerge with an identical tube. That done, they moved to load the first tub into the back of the van and that was when Sean called in his men. In a matter of seconds they had them covered from all angles.

"Don't move!" Sean told them, his gun trained on Kurt. When Kurt saw him, his face took on a deadly expression. Sean knew he wasn't going down without a fight, and he was about to give him one. Suddenly Kurt drew his gun, firing at him. Sean took cover by the side of the van, returning fire. Then all hell broke loose as both sides fired at each other. Sean could see Jack opposite him behind a post as he fired at the boat. Jack signaled to him, to cover the other end of the van. Sean spun and went around the van, taking down the driver as he came at him firing like crazy. From where he was Sean could see Kurt making a run for it down the dark side of the docks. He went after him. Sean glanced back to see Jack not far behind. Kurt stopped firing at him. Sean took cover. As he glanced back at Jack, he saw a man coming up on him. He signaled Jack, who turned, taking the man down. Sean was up and after Kurt as he watched him disappear into the warehouse ahead. Sean followed with caution. Inside the semidark warehouse, moonlight streaming through the high large glass windows gave him some visibility. Barrels and crates of all sizes filled the room. Sean glanced behind him to Jack. He signaled for Jack to cover the other side.

Sean could feel his adrenaline rise as he ventured farther inside. Suddenly he heard the rumble sound and looked up to see a barrel falling towards him. As Sean dove out of the way,

Kurt came out from hiding, firing at him. Sean slammed hard into a crate. A sharp pain ripped through his shoulder, but he was up and firing. He saw Kurt running and went after him. Kurt fired blindly as he ran. Sean chased after him, dodging the wild bullets as they came at him.

"Freeze!" He aimed his gun at him, firing a warning shot. Kurt didn't stop. Sean could have killed him, he had a good enough shot, but he wanted him alive. Kurt kept going. Sean shot him in the leg. Kurt went down screaming. Jack came out to cover Kurt. Sean gestured for Jack to stay back. Kurt had a gun on him. And from his curled up position on the floor, there was no telling what he might do. He was still screaming and holding his wounded leg.

"Don't move!" Sean warned. Kurt let out strings of curses, spitting at him.

"Let me see yu' gun," Sean demanded.

"Yu' dead!" Kurt screamed at him. Kurt was sweating. Sean could see the blood flowing through his fingers over his wound. And that was when Kurt went wild. He growled like a madman, pushing himself up, firing at him. Sean fired back, hitting him in the chest twice. Jack also fired, hitting Kurt in the back. Kurt went down, dead. Sean walked over to him. He lay on his side, eyes wide open. His gun was still in his hand. Sean kicked the gun out of his hand. He didn't want it to end like this, but Kurt had given them no other choice.

"Yu' OK?" Jack asked, looking at him.

"Yeah," he said, looking at Kurt's body.

Jack walked over to him and took his arm, looking at it. He felt the pain in his arm and looked down at it. He'd been shot. From the look of it, it was only a flesh wound. One of Kurt's bullets must have hit him when he slammed into the crates. He pulled out his handkerchief and pressed it against the wound to stop the bleeding. They had the drugs and had taken Kurt down but he still wasn't satisfied. He wanted Mike; however, more than that, he needed Kelee.

Back at the docks Sean gave his men specific instructions about securing the drugs, the boat, and the arrest of the men they hadn't killed. Sean then called his cousin Sue, who was a doctor, asking her to meet him at the safe house.

Jack looked at him and smiled. "Guess I'll drive."

Chapter 15

Kelee came awake suddenly. Disoriented, she looked about the room, recalling that Sean had her locked up. She closed her eyes and that was when she heard the voices. She threw off her covers and jumped out of bed, slipping her feet into her bed slippers. She headed downstairs. She heard a few male voices and a woman's. She walked into the living room to see a small pretty woman hovering over a shirtless Sean. She was doing something to his arm, but she couldn't see what.

"Yu' should know better," the woman scolded Sean, who moaned. Kris stood nearby watching whatever the woman was doing to Sean. Kelee saw Jack coming out of the kitchen with a couple of stouts. Jack saw her and cleared his throat. Everyone looked at her. Kelee's eyes met Sean's. He looked like he was in pain and that was when she saw what the woman was doing to him. She was stitching up a nasty-looking gash on his left arm. She also saw bloody gauze in a bowl on the sofa and her heart sank. He'd been hurt. Fear gripped her. He'd been hurt, was all she could think of.

"Kelee?" Sean said. She looked at him, afraid. "I'm OK, it's a flesh wound." He gave her a reassuring smile.

"Keep still!" the woman warned, finishing her stitching. Kelee remained frozen. She found that she couldn't speak.

"Kelee, this is my cousin Dr. Sue Harrold; Sue, Kelee," Sean introduced them. Sue looked her over.

"So yu' the reason he didn't want to go to the hospital." Sue smiled at her. "I can see why," she said. "Just don't do this again; next time yu' might get an infection," she warned and finished her stitching. She cleaned his wound and put a dressing on it. Then she pulled off her gloves and packed her small doctor's bag. She pulled out some fresh dressings, leaving them on the sofa.

"Yu' need to change the dressin' once a day," Sue told Sean.

She walked over to Kelee and looked her right in the eyes.

"Take care of him; he needs it," Sue told her and left. Jack and Kris left the room also.

"Sorry we woke yu'," Sean said, moving over to her. She stared at his naked chest; he had such a fantastic body. She suppressed her desires;

there were more important things to address.
Like how he got wounded. She could still see the
bloodstain on his jeans. It was his blood and it
made her heart race with fear. Kelee stared at
him, not knowing what to say.

"Have yu' been shot before?" She couldn't
recall seeing any scars on his body, and then
again, she hadn't seen every inch of him.

"Yeah," he admitted.

"Where?"

"In the thigh, another flesh wound," he told
her with a smile. She didn't find it funny. He
lived a dangerous life. His work was dangerous. Being with him was dangerous. She wondered if him getting shot had anything to do
with the kidnapping.

"What's really going on, Sean? I need to
know." She heard her voice tremble. She was
scared.

"Don't be frightened," he told her, taking her
into his arms, holding her tightly against him. It
felt wonderful to be in his arms, but also scary.

"I want to go home," she told him, trying not
to cry.

"I can't let yu' go, not yet," he said, kissing the
top of her head. She looked up at him.

"Why?"

"Yu' safer here," he said. She could see regret
in his eyes.

"From who, Sean?"

His eyes held such conflict that Kelee trembled. Was it that bad? Whatever it was, she needed to know.

"Please, Sean, I need to know," she said and pulled away from him. He looked at her, torn.

"Come with me," he said, taking her hand. He led her upstairs and into the room adjacent to hers. The room was a little bigger than hers and had the same kind of furniture.

Kelee watched as Sean got out of the bloody jeans. He wore boxers; she went hot at the sight of him. He had great muscular legs. She reminded herself that she should be mad at him, but looking at him she felt relieved that he was OK. She sat against the headboard and wrapped her arms around her knees. She watched him as he washed up in the adjoining bathroom. He returned, wiping his face with a towel. He sat on the edge of the bed and gazed at her with that torn expression again. He looked tired.

"I'm sorry for lyin' to yu'. I never meant to hurt yu'," he started. "This isn't the way I want 'tings between us. I especially don't want to keep yu' locked up here, but yu' safety is important to me. I don't want any'ting to happen to yu'." His sincerity touched her. She wanted to touch him, kiss him, but she was too scared.

"I've been after this dealer name Mike Curve for about three years. He's a ruthless businessman and a killer," Sean said. "He uses his business connections to traffic drugs. Every time we get some'ting on him, he slips by us. But this time, I've got him and I'm goin' to take him down. He has eyes everywhere. That's why we haven't been able to get him. That guy Tyce who came to yu' rescue is one of Curve's men."

Kelee covered her mouth with her hands, trembling. "Oh my God!"

"I'm sure he arranged yu' gettin' robbed that day."

Kelee thought back to how it had all went down that day and realized that Sean was right. The whole idea of Tyce watching her and pretending to be her friend disgusted her. She had almost played right into his trap, especially back at the west coast. She felt like a fool.

"Don't beat yu'self up about it. I just found out who he really is."

Kelee smiled, grateful for Sean and the fact that he was protecting her. She looked at his wound and wondered how hurt he was.

"How did that happen?"

"I had to take down Curve's brother tonight."

"Is he dead?" She was almost afraid to ask.

"He gave me no choice. That means 'tings will be dangerous until I get Curve. That's why yu' here. His people have seen us together and I don't want any'ting to happen to yu'." He took her hand. She moved to him, wrapping her arms around his neck. She knew she'd always be safe with him.

"I understand now," she told him.

"Forgive me." He pressed his lips against her cheek.

"When this is over I expect yu' to do some major apologizing, especially for this kidnapping bit. Yu' scared the hell out of me." She gazed into his beautiful eyes.

"Sorry; so can I start apologizin' now?" he asked with his sexy smirk.

"Yu' hurt," she reminded him, looking at his wound.

"Not where it matters." He gestured to his crotch. She looked down to see him bulging out of his shorts. She smiled and giggled like a schoolgirl, touching him. He was warm and hard in her hand. He moaned at her touch, pulling her towards him, kissing her. She melted under his kiss. He pulled her down under him, never breaking their kiss. His hand found and caressed her breasts through her silk PJ top. Her body trembled with her need for him. She moaned, tightening her hold on him, careful not to touch his wound. He pulled back, admiring her. She looked at the open bedroom door, and he got up, closing the door and turning the light off. The bright moonlight illuminated the room. She sat up and started to unbutton her PJ top. He sat on the edge of the bed watching her. He smiled as she tossed the top aside. He reached for her PJ bottom and pulled it off. He ran his hand up her leg and up her inner thigh to rest on her pelvis. His touch elevated her desire as she trembled under his touch. He pulled her underwear off, admiring her body. He got up and pulled off his underwear and reached for a condom in the drawer before rejoining her on the bed. She opened her arms and legs to him. She welcomed him inside her, and into her heart. Their lovemaking was a slow exploration that left them spent. They fell asleep in each other's arms as dawn crept into the skies.

Chapter 16

Kelee woke to find Sean still sleeping beside her. She had thought he'd have left, but he was still here with her. She watched him sleep for a while. He looked so at peace. She studied him, knowing it would be hard when she left St. Pala. She was going to miss him, but she would enjoy every moment with him.

Sean's eyes slowly opened; she smiled at him; he reached for her, pulling her on top of him. Their lips met in a heated kiss that left her hungry and wanting more. She wrapped her arms around him, rubbing her pelvis against his hardening sex. His hands gripped her rear, pressing her hard against him. She trailed kisses down his chest and across his stomach; she pulled back and took his sex in her hands, caressing him. He closed his eyes and moaned her name. Reaching for a condom, she luxuriously put it on him, enjoying the pleasure she was giving him. She saddled him and exhaled as she took him inside her, falling onto his chest, moaning his name. He grasped her hips, lifting and lowering her on him. In one fluid movement Sean had her on her back and was moving hard and fast against her. She held on to him, moaning his name as they both found the ultimate release together.

Kelee must have dozed off because when she woke, Sean was gone. For a moment she was disappointed, but smiled as she remembered their night and morning together. She got up, took a shower and went downstairs for something to eat.

Kris was sitting on a chair, smoking in the backyard. He gave her a nod and a smile, enjoying his cigarette.

Kelee made a large cheese omelet with toast. She was pouring coffee when Sean walked into the kitchen looking refreshed. He was dressed in loose slacks and a white undershirt. He smiled at Kelee, moved over to her and pulled her into his arms, kissing her. She returned his kiss, enjoying the minty taste of him.

"Mornin'." He smiled, releasing her. She smiled up at him.

"Mornin'. Hungry?" she asked.

"Yeah, thanks," he said and took the plate she offered with half of the large omelet and toast. It was good to have him here with her like this, but she also knew he'd be gone soon. His work was far from done. Yes, he had killed the dealer's brother, but what about the dealer?

"Are yu' goin' after this dealer?" she asked. Sean stopped eating and looked at her.

"I have to," he said. The determination in his eyes scared her. She knew he was doing his job, and it scared the hell out of her.

"Is yu' work always this dangerous?"

"No," he said. "I usually don't get this physically involved, but this case is different. The police haven't been able to get to Curve. That's why I was called in."

"Oh." She was afraid for him. She had thought dating a possessive cop was bad, but this was worse. Sean's work had put both of them in danger. She wasn't sure if she could really deal with it.

"It's goin' to be OK. I promise," he reassured her, taking her hand. She looked into his eyes. She believed him, but she also wanted to get away from it all. It was a bit too much for her right now.

Kris entered the kitchen and Sean let go of her hand.

"Jack called," Kris told Sean.

Sean got up from the table and went to make his call. Kelee started to clear the table. She knew he'd be gone again. She hated the fact that he had to go after Curve, but he had a job to do. A few minutes later Sean returned and from the look on his face she knew he'd be leaving.

"I have to go," he announced, walking over to her. Kris had gone back outside.

"Be careful," she said, holding back her tears. He walked over to her, taking her face in his hands and looking into her eyes.

"I promise, this will be over soon." He kissed her long and hard. Kelee felt alone and scared as she watched him leave.

Tyce was a nervous wreck. Kurt was dead and he had to tell Mike. Mike had told him to take care of Kurt, but Kurt was hotheaded and reckless. Kurt was supposed to come in at the west docks and at the last minute had changed the location and fallen right into Sean's hands. Knowing Mike, he would want someone to pay for Kurt's death, and it wasn't going to be him. He had to deliver big and he knew exactly what he had to do to keep Mike from killing him for Kurt's death.

Back at his office Sean was informed that Mike was back in St. Pala. No one knew exactly where he was, but he was back on the island. Which meant he had come back sometime in the morning. This also meant that he knew of his brother's death. He was going to come after him with everything he had, but Sean was prepared for him.

* * *

Kelee was about to take a shower when the cell phone rang. She answered it, expecting to hear Sean's voice. She missed him terribly and was worried about him.

"Kelee?" Allan's panicked voice came over the phone. Instantly a cold chill ran through her.

"What happened?" Her voiced trembled in fear as both Lori and Sean flashed before her eyes.

"It's Lori," Allan said.

"Oh, God, is she OK?"

"She was in an accident. I don't know how bad it is yet."

"What kind of accident?"

"I don't know, I'm about an hour way from town," Allan told her.

"Which hospital is she in?"

"Kings Hill. Is Sean with yu'?"

"No," Kelee told him.

"Can yu' get to the hospital? I don't want her alone."

"I'll be there; see yu' soon," Kelee reassured him.

Kelee pulled out a pair of jeans, a T-shirt, and her flats and hurried downstairs. She found Kris watching TV.

"Yu' have to take me to the hospital! My sister was in an accident and she needs me," she told him frantically.

"Sorry, I can't," he told her. Kelee glared at him, boiling mad.

"Listen, my sister is pregnant and hurt and she needs me. I don't care what Sean told yu,' I'm goin' to that hospital. After I see that my sister is OK, yu' can bring me back here. My sister needs me, and yu' taking me right now!" she demanded.

Kris looked at her, torn.

"Please, I jus' need to make sure that she's OK. Please, she needs me."

"I can take yu', but we can't stay too long," Kris told her.

"Thank yu'," she told him, relieved.

The car Kris took her to the hospital in had tinted windows, added security no doubt. She noted that the drive took almost forty-five minutes. She also noted that the house was located in a country area with widespread farmlands.

The hospital Lori was at was uptown. It was a small private hospital with peach-tiled floors. The nurse told them what room Lori was in. Kelee and Kris took the elevator to the maternity ward on the third floor. Kelee rushed into the room. Kris stayed outside. Lori was lying in the bed, asleep. Kelee noted the bruise on her forehead. She rushed to Lori's side.

"Lori?"

Slowly Lori opened her eyes and smiled at her.

"Yu' OK?"

Lori smiled. "Yeah, I panicked. The baby isn't comin'."

Kelee hugged and kissed her, relieved. "Thank God."

"The doctor wants to monitor me for a few more hours before he sends me home." Lori looked her over. "Are yu' OK? Is he treatin' yu' well?"

Kelee smiled. "Yes."

"I'm surprise he let yu' out of his sight."

"He doesn't know. I convinced Kris, the guy who's watchin' me, to bring me to see yu'."

"Sorry I scared yu'." Lori pushed herself up into a better sitting position. Kelee adjusted her pillows for her.

"I'm just happy yu' OK. Did Allan get to yu'?"

"Yes, he's not far away." Lori sighed, tired.

"How did yu' get into an accident?"

"My fault. I backed out into this guy's car."

"Is the guy OK?"

"Yeah, thank God. Allan's gonna be so mad at me. He doesn't want me to drive, yu' know."

"No, he won't," Kelee told her with a reassuring smile. "He'll be happy yu' OK."

Kelee recalled Allan telling her sister numerous times that she needed to have someone drive her in her state. Kelee felt guilty for not being there for her sister. Her whole reason for coming to St. Pala was to be with her. She had made a mistake and that was getting involved with Sean. It was starting to cost her. She was under lockdown and now her sister could have done serious damage to herself because she wasn't there for her.

"It really shouldn't be like this; getting involved with Sean is costing me too much."

"It will be over soon," Lori reassured her.

"Yu' right about that one," a voice said behind them. Kelee recognized the voice and a shiver raced down her spine. She turned to see Tyce just behind Kris. Tyce shoved Kris into the room, closing the door behind him. Kelee's eyes fell to the gun Tyce had in his hand with the silencer attached.

"Oh, God!" Lori gasped.

"Not a sound," Tyce warned. Kelee grasped her sister's hand. Fear gripped her, making her numb.

Kelee saw another gun at Tyce's waist. She recognized it as Kris's gun. Kelee gazed at Kris, who was looking at her. He had a look of dread on his face. This was not good. She shouldn't have let Kris bring her here. She had put them all in danger.

"I knew she'd bring yu' outta hidin'." Tyce smiled, looking at her. Kelee looked at Lori, alarmed, then at Tyce.

"Yu' caused the accident?" she asked, angry. "Yu' could have killed her an' her unborn child, yu' ass!" Kelee was outraged.

"If I wanted her dead, she'd be dead an' that goes for yu,' too." His deadly tone scared Kelee.

"What do yu' want?" Lori asked, afraid. He saw the fear in Lori's eyes and smiled.

"Her." He smiled at Kelee with a smirk.

"No!" Lori cried, holding on to Kelee's hand tightly. Tyce pointed the gun at Lori.

"Yu' need to keep quiet!" He glared. Lori started to cry.

"It's OK," Kelee reassured her sister.

"Let's go!" Tyce demanded.

Kelee looked at him, unable to move.

"Yu' don't come with me, I'll kill her," he said and pointed the gun at Lori. Kelee felt her heart stop. She bent and kissed her sister's cheek.

"Tell Sean to come get me," she whispered to Lori.

Suddenly Kris lunged at Tyce. There was a soft pop and Kris fell backwards. Lori covered her mouth, stifling her scream. Kelee felt like she would vomit when she saw the blood pouring from Kris's chest. She watched as Kris's eyes rolled back into his head and he went still. He'd killed Kris. Suddenly the seriousness of the situation hit her. Tyce would kill her, Lori, and her unborn child if she didn't do what he wanted. She couldn't let him harm Lori and her unborn child. Tyce pointed his gun back at Kelee.

"Now!" he demanded with a deadly look in his eyes.

Suddenly Allan's voice calling for Lori came from outside the door. Kelee wanted to call out to Allan, but she knew it would be a mistake. Tyce had a gun and he would use it.

"No, Allan," she heard Lori cry. Kelee kept her eye fixed on the door. Quickly Tyce positioned himself behind the door.

"Please don't," Kelee whispered and Tyce glared at her.

Allan came through the door in a hurry. Kelee shook her head no at him, but he didn't notice. Allan was totally focused on Lori.

Tyce shoved the door closed. Just before Allan could turn Tyce slammed the butt of the gun on the back of his head. Allan fell to the floor unconscious.

"Allan," Lori gasped, crying louder now. Kelee turned to her, brushing her tears away.

"He'll be fine." She kissed her cheek.

"Kelee." Lori clung to her.

"Let's go!" Tyce demanded, waving the gun at her.

Kelee let go of Lori and walked towards Tyce. He grabbed her, putting his arms around her waist and sticking the gun in her side. The still warm gun nozzle penetrated her shirt. Tyce shoved Allan's unconscious body with his foot out of the way. Kelee glanced back at a crying Lori as Tyce led her from the room. She prayed to God she'd see them again.

"Don't make any sudden move," Tyce whispered in her ear as they came off the elevator. Kelee nodded and held back her tears. This was not happening to her. This was crazy. She shouldn't have left the house; she should have listened to Sean.

The nurse looked up at them as they passed her station. She couldn't see the gun, but Kelee wasn't about to take any risk with Tyce. She had seen him kill Kris. He would kill her, she knew that, and she wasn't ready to die.

Tyce led her outside and towards a black SUV with tinted windows. He opened the back door. "Get in," he demanded. She did as she was told. "Slide over," he told he as he got in beside her. A mean-looking Indian sat behind the wheel. He grinned at her through the rearview mirror. Kelee cringed in fear, her mind reeling with thoughts of what they would probably do to her.

"Go!" Tyce told the driver and the man took off. Kelee sat as far away from Tyce as she could get. He still had his gun trained on her. She stared out the window, wondering where they were taking her. They were heading downtown, that much she knew. Kelee closed her eyes and prayed that Sean would find her.

"Talk to me," Tyce said and she looked at him, annoyed.

"What for?" she spat at him, unable to hide her anger. The driver laughed and Tyce jammed the gun in the back of his neck.

"Shut up!" he snarled at the driver, who instantly became very serious. Tyce looked at her; Kelee glared at him.

"I thought we were friends," Tyce appealed to her, but she wasn't fooled.

"Yu' call setting me up at the crafts market, threatening my family and my life friendship? Are yu' kidding me?"

Tyce looked at her, surprised.

"By the way, what did yu' do with my sister's car?"

"That's the least of yu' worries," he said in such a cold tone, Kelee trembled.

"What yu' intend to do to me?"

He smiled and looked her over. Kelee got very nervous. Did he intend to rape her? Oh, God, she prayed Sean would find her.

"It's not yu' he wants," Tyce told her and Kelee looked at him, alarmed. "Knowin' Sean, he'll come after yu' and when he does, he's dead and yu' can go back to New York to yu' decoratin'."

Kelee's heart raced with fear. They were going to kill Sean. Sean would come after her, she knew that and they knew that. They'd kill him, because of her. She should not have left the house. Kelee felt the tears well up in her eyes and roll down her cheeks.

Chapter 17

Sean felt like his entire world had been ripped out from under him. They had Kelee. The one thing he knew was that he had to find her fast before she came to any harm. He was the one Mike wanted, not Kelee. He also knew Mike intended to use Kelee to get to him. Sean also had a gut feeling that Mike would kill Kelee; after all, he had killed Kurt. Why the hell had she left the safe house? He looked at a sobbing Lori in the hospital bed and knew exactly why. He felt bad about the whole situation. Kelee had come here to be with her sister, and he had taken her away from Lori. Now they had taken Kelee from him. She was in grave danger and it was his fault. He had to get her back; she didn't deserve this. Lori didn't deserve this, either, having her sister snatched away from her like this.

"He took her," Lori kept repeating as tears streamed down her face. Allan was trying his best to calm Lori down, but Lori was too hysterical.

This wasn't good for her in her present state. Sean was glad that Allan wasn't hurt, either.

Kris was currently in surgery from being shot. The bullet had missed his heart, but he wasn't out of danger yet. Sean prayed he'd make it and come out all right, but right now he had to find Kelee.

"Please find her," Lori begged him. "She told me to tell yu' to come for her. Please, Sean, find her."

The rage that filled Sean was starting to consume him. Mike had Kelee and it complicated everything. Suddenly he felt like he was about to lose it, but he had to stay focused. He wasn't about to lose Kelee.

Sean walked over to Lori and kissed her cheek. "I will, I promise," he told her and quickly left the room. He was halfway down the hall when Allan caught up with him.

"Wha' yu' goin' to do?" Allan asked, rubbing the lump at the back of his head.

"Get Kelee back an' get rid of him once an' for all," Sean told him in a dry, deadly tone.

"Be careful. If yu' need any'ting. . . ."

"Thanks, but for now, jus' take care of Lori, keep her calm," Sean said and hurried off.

Jack was waiting for him outside. Sean jumped into the jeep and Jack took off.

"Is everyone ready?"

"Yeah," Jack said.

The minute Sean had learned that Mike had

Kelee he had called an emergency meeting; they were now heading to his office for the meeting.

"Yu' OK?" Jack asked. Sean had been staring out the window into passing traffic, thinking of Kelee, praying she was OK.

"Yeah." Sean's brain was working overtime trying to figure out where Mike might have taken Kelee. He had numerous businesses and homes in St. Pala. Sean didn't know where to start.

"We'll find her," Jack reassured him. Sean took as much comfort as he could in Jack's words, but he was also prepared for the worst.

At his office, the commissioner, Frank Tam, and Assistant Superintendent Paul Thomas were waiting for him. Sean immediately briefed them on the situation.

"I want every'ting Mike Curve owns raided. I want her found and I want her found alive," he insisted. "If yu' have to take Curve down, do it 'cause he will kill any of us."

"Yu' talkin' massive manpower, yu' know that?" Tam said with a smirk.

"No'ting yu' can't handle," Sean told him.

"Yu' got that right." Thomas grinned.

They all had a common interest and that was to get rid of Curve. Sean was glad he had their support.

"Just remember one 'ting," Sean injected. "I want her back safe."

"We'll find her," Tam reassured him.

"Thanks." Sean sighed.

Kelee was taken to a house somewhere in the middle of downtown. Tyce pulled her out of the jeep. Kelee cringed in fear at the sight of the place. This was one part of St. Pala she never thought she'd ever see. It was a rough ghetto area, more than likely known for its violent setting. She noted the decaying homes, some no more than shacks. Zinc fences surrounded most of the homes. The streets were small and in bad disarray. Sewer water ran in the gutters, giving off a godawful scent. Rough-looking men hung on the streets, watching them. It was starting to get dark and Kelee trembled in fear as Tyce led her through a rusty iron gate that screeched into a paved yard. He took her towards a small red house that looked remarkably good for the kind of neighborhood they were in. The small veranda was polished a bright red, the front door of the house had old glazed glass panels. Just as they reached the door a short tough-looking woman, dripping in gold and dressed in the lasted hot fashion, opened it. She was olive skinned with a crazy up-do. She smiled, flashing gold-capped front teeth at Tyce. The woman looked Kelee over with interest. Her eyes weren't threatening, which eased her discomfort a bit.

"Monica, I need yu' to hold her for a few

hours," Tyce said and pushed Kelee into a small, overdecorated, and very clean living room. Tyce shoved her into a still plastic-covered armchair. He gave her a warning look; Kelee glared back at him.

"I wouldn't even 'tink of it," he said with a smirk. "Yu wouldn't make it a foot past the front gate."

Kelee knew he was right; she sank into the chair, defeated. In this type of neighborhood she stuck out like a sore thumb, which made her a target. Tyce pulled out a wad of cash from his pocket and handed it to a very happy Monica.

"I'll be back in a couple of hours," he told Monica and left.

"Want some'ting to drink?"

Kelee looked at her, surprised. "Thank yu'." Kelee gave her a slight smile. Monica disappeared through a curtained doorway. Kelee looked around the room. She noticed family pictures of Monica, an older woman, and two young boys who resembled Monica. She also noticed a picture of Monica and Tyce. They were smiling; she wondered what the connection between them was. Monica returned with a bottled soda. Kelee took it from her, thanking her.

"So, wha' yu' do to vex Tyce?" Monica asked in a serious tone.

"He's the one who kidnapped me and almost killed my sister and her unborn child," Kelee told her, upset. Monica paused and looked at her, surprised.

"He must be doin' this for C, then," Monica said.

"Who's C?" Kelee asked.

"Someone yu' don't want to mess with," Monica said, shaking her head. Suddenly Kelee realized that she was talking about Mike Curve. Kelee trembled in fear.

"Can yu' help me?" Kelee asked, unable to hide the fear in her eyes.

"Sorry, can't; I value my life. Yu' know wha' I mean?"

Kelee nodded, understanding. They had Monica in the palm of their hands, much like they did her. Kelee closed her eyes, squeezing back her tears. Would Sean even find her in time? She had to have faith he would.

Chapter 18

Raids were conducted on every business and home that Mike Curve and Tyce Thomas owed. They found nothing. Tyce had somehow disappeared; he hadn't left the island, that much Sean knew. He had the airport covered. If Tyce made any attempt to leave the island, he'd be arrested. Three hours had passed since Tyce took Kelee and no one had seen them. This was not good. Sean was starting to get desperate and it wasn't an emotion he liked. He knew one thing for sure: he intended to make Curve and Tyce pay for everything they had done.

Tyce returned exactly two hours later, only this time he wore a dreadlock wig and was dressed in jeans and a T-shirt. He had changed his appearance because he knew Sean was looking for them. Kelee took some comfort in that. Again, she prayed he'd find her. The same jeep and driver were waiting outside when Tyce led her from the house. It was dark outside, which meant they'd be harder to spot. She wondered where he was taking her as they drove out of the neighborhood and back onto the main street, heading farther downtown.

Tyce pulled off the wig and rubbed his head. She looked at the wig, then at him.

"I guess Sean has people lookin' for me," she said with some satisfaction. Tyce glared at her.

"We'll make sure he knows where yu' are, an' when he comes for yu', we'll take care of him." Tyce smiled wickedly. She trembled in fear; Sean was going to walk into a trap because of her.

Kelee was taken to a secluded decaying dock area where a small yacht waited. The yacht looked like it had seen better days. Tyce hurried her onto the boat and she was shoved below and locked in a musty bedroom. The room held a bed and built-in storage units. There were no windows, so she had no idea where she was being taken. Moments later she heard the engines of the yacht start up and felt it surge forward. It came to a stop about fifteen minutes later and she heard Tyce's footsteps as he came below. Kelee sat on the edge of the bed, praying he wouldn't hurt her. They were the only two on the yacht and she had no way of escaping him. Her heart raced as he opened the door and entered. He had hand-cuffs in one hand. Kelee sat quiet, trying not to panic. He walked over to her, grabbed her hands and slapped the handcuffs on her. Kelee looked down at the silver metal on her hand.

"Why the cuffs?" she asked as calm as she could.

"Just in case yu' decide to take a swim." He grinned.

"I think we are too far for that, don't yu' think?"

"Yes, but yu' never know." He pulled her to her feet.

Sean got the call just as he was about to leave his office. A dread was spotted with a woman fitting Kelee's description near the decaying east docks. Immediately he called the coast guard to watch out and track the yacht.

Sean hurried toward Jack's office. Jack was just hanging up the phone. "They spotted a yacht heading south; let's load up," Sean told Jack, who was on his feet instantly. They headed towards the equipment room, loading up on guns and ammunition. Sean was taking no chances.

At the docks a coast guard speedboat waited for them. Sean and Jack got on board. At the helm was Lieutenant Green, a short, stout black man in his mid-thirties.

"They spotted the yacht headin' towards Maze Island," Green told them over the roar of the engine as the boat bounced on the waves.

Maze was a small secluded island; the only

thing there was an old mansion some billionaire had built ten years ago. The billionaire had died some five years ago and the mansion was abandoned. Maze Island wasn't linked to St. Pala, so whatever went on there he had no jurisdiction over.

Fifteen minutes later they came upon the west end of Maze Island. The top of the mansion could be seen through the trees in the middle of the island. There was a small yacht and a speedboat in the dock. Through binoculars Sean surveyed the shoreline; he didn't see any movement. They pulled into the dock.

"Stay here, and radio for backup," Sean told Green. Green immediately got on the radio.

Sean and Jack, guns drawn, got off the boat and headed ashore with caution.

Chapter 19

Kelee sat on the edge of the naked mattress on the sledge bed, the only piece of furniture in the room that Tyce had locked her in. She rubbed her wrist, grateful Tyce had removed the cuffs. She recalled everything she saw on her way here after they had gotten off the yacht. There was a rough stone path that led from the docks about a mile to the vacant mansion.

She went to the window, trying it again, and that was when she noticed it was nailed shut. Through the dirty glass windows she could see an empty backyard pool and a helicopter on a small landing strip. She saw Tyce and another man unload a long slim crate from the helicopter. The man was taller and bigger than Tyce. She wondered if he was Mike Curve. The man wore a baseball cap, so she couldn't make out his face. She watched them until they disappeared out of her sight.

Kelee decided to try the door again. She rattled it when it wouldn't open, then she heard a click to her surprise and it opened. Kelee paused for a moment and thought of her next move. If she could make it back to the docks, then maybe she could get on the yacht and get back to St. Pala. She didn't know how to drive a boat, but she couldn't just sit here. The shoreline was still visible; she recalled as much, as Tyce had dragged her from the yacht earlier.

Cautiously Kelee left the room. She quickly looked around, and hurried as quietly as she could down the stairs. The front door was ajar; she made a run for it. Suddenly she was yanked backwards by her hair, spun around and slammed into the hard wall. She screamed as the back of her head collided with the wall; she saw stars. A hand clasped her neck and she screamed, kicking at her assailant, the man in the cap. He was a dark, hard-looking man with hazel eyes. He scared the hell out of her. Then he slapped her so hard her ears buzzed. The entire left side of her face stung so badly, she became dizzy and her knees started to buckle. His hand around her neck kept her upright, but also left her gasping for air. Tears spilled down her cheeks.

"Please let me go," she cried and he slapped her harder this time. Kelee tasted blood in her mouth.

"I want yu' to go back to yu' room, an' if yu' leave that room, I will kill yu'!" His eyes blazed at her. She trembled in fear knowing he meant every word he said. Kelee started crying, she couldn't help it. The man released her and Kelee had to brace herself against the wall to steady her nerves.

Tyce walked into the hall then. His eyes immediately met and held hers; he looked at her with a blank expression. Kelee cradled her bruised face and headed back upstairs and back into the room. She closed the door behind her and fell onto the bed crying.

"Please, God, let Sean find me," she prayed.

Sean and Jack surveyed the mansion from behind the bushes. They hadn't seen any movement in the past few minutes. They had come up on the side of the mansion, which was concealed by shrubs. It was a great cover for them.

"I'm goin' 'round back," Sean told Jack.

"I got the other side." Jack nodded. Sean quickly ran up to the side of the mansion. He glanced behind him to see Jack disappearing around the other side of the house. Sean proceeded with caution. At the back of the house he spotted the helicopter sitting on a platform about ten feet from the empty pool. He surveyed the area. He didn't see anyone. Sean noticed that a long crate held the back door of the mansion open. He wondered what was in it. They had to be inside the house, which kind of complicated things. He didn't know the layout of the house or how many of them were in there. Jack came up on the other side of the house and nodded to him. Sean signaled to the door. Cautiously they approached the open door. The kitchen was dusty and decaying. Sean noted a number of crates and moved over to them. He easily opened one of the boxes and was shocked at what was inside: M-16 rifles. So Curve had gone from running drugs to guns.

"So it's guns now," Jack whispered to him.

Sean checked for ammunition; there was none. He noted that the serial numbers were scratched off the guns, so there was no way they could be traced. Sean wasn't about to let Curve traffic any of these weapons into St. Pala. He wondered where else Curve was selling the guns.

Just then they heard footsteps. They immediately took cover. Jack moved behind the door and Sean behind the kitchen aisle. Tyce walked into the kitchen and Jack was instantly in his face, gun pointed right at his head. Tyce froze. Jack dragged Tyce farther into the kitchen. Sean was on him in a second.

"Where is she?" He jammed his gun in Tyce's jaw. Tyce laughed and Sean slammed the butt of his gun against Tyce's head. The blow stunned him and he staggered. Tyce gave him a murderous look. Sean hit him again, this time hard, busting his lip.

"I said, where is she?"

Suddenly Sean heard a scream. He instantly knew it was Kelee. He released the safety off his gun.

"She's upstairs, first room on the left," Tyce told him quickly. Sean gazed at Jack.

"Go, I got him," Jack said. Sean ran into the living room. He quickly cased the room, which was empty, and like the kitchen, dusty. Sean noticed numerous footprints. He wondered who else was in the house. They'd only seen Tyce, but there were a number of different size footprints outlined on the dusty wooden floors.

"Get away from me!" he heard Kelee scream and he ran upstairs, kicking in the first door on the left. What he saw stopped him cold in his tracks. Penn had a hold of Kelee's arm and she was trying to get away from him. Penn looked at him and smiled, relieved.

"Sean," Kelee said, glad to see him. He was glad to see that she was OK.

"Thank God yu' here," she said, moving towards Sean. Sean looked at a frightened Kelee. She had a large bruise on her right cheek. Sean instantly pointed his gun at Penn. While Sean was relieved to see him alive, something wasn't right.

"Hey, hey, I jus' came to get the girl." Penn held his hands up. "Curve said she was up here, an', an'," he stuttered.

Sean could see that Penn was trying to make something up.

"Where's Curve?"

"He's downstairs," Penn said quickly.

"Where were yu'?" Something wasn't right here.

"He had me locked up?" Penn said. Sean studied Penn. He had unusually clean clothes for someone who had been missing for weeks and locked up. Instantly Sean knew he was the one. Penn was the one who Curve had in his pocket. No wonder Curve was always a step ahead of him.

Suddenly Penn made for Kelee. Kelee screamed and jumped onto the bed. Penn pulled a gun from his waist in the process. Sean reacted in a split second. The first shot hit Penn in the shoulder. Shocked, Penn looked at his wound, then at Sean in disbelief. Penn raised his gun at him.

"Don't do this, man," Sean told him. Penn laughed, and continued to raise his gun. The second bullet hit Penn in the chest. Penn laughed; then he fell to his knees, then dropped dead onto his face.

Seconds later Kelee was in his arms crying and thanking him for coming for her. Sean held her close as she cried. He didn't feel right about any of this. He'd just had to kill one of his best men, who had betrayed him. This just wasn't right, but he had threatened Kelee's life and he'd sworn to protect her.

"Are yu' OK? Did they hurt yu'?" Sean asked, putting Kelee away from him.

"No, no," she cried.

He wiped the tears from her eyes. He could see the fear still in her eyes and it tore at his heart. He kissed her long and hard; she clung to him, returning his kiss. It felt so good to have her safe and in his arms. But he also knew it wasn't over until he got Curve and got Kelee off this island.

Suddenly Sean heard gunshots. Kelee gasped, clinging to him.

"Jack," Sean said. He looked around the room; there was no other way out. Taking Kelee's hand, he led her from the room with caution. In the hall Sean turned to Kelee. "I want yu' to find somewhere to hide."

"Please don't leave me," she cried, frightened. It tore at his heart. He took a hold of her face and looked into her eyes. "Yu' have to find somewhere safe until I come back for yu', understand?"

She nodded. He hated leaving her, but he had to make sure Jack was OK. Plus, Curve was still here and there was no way he was getting away from him.

Sean turned to go downstairs when he heard Kelee scream. Sean felt a sense of dread. He reacted instantly, turning, gun drawn. But he already had her. Curve had Kelee in a choke hold with a gun at her head. Sean's eyes met and held Kelee's. He saw only fear in her tear-filled eyes.

"Let her go, Curve!" Sean demanded.

Curve tightened his arm around Kelee's throat. She started to gag. Sean didn't have a clear shot. If he didn't do something Curve's hold on Kelee would kill her. He had used that kind of choke hold on numerous criminals; it could be fatal. Tears rolled down Kelee's cheeks.

"Sean," she cried. His heart raced with fear of losing her. But he had no intention of losing her, not today.

"Let her go, Curve!" Sean demanded, trying to find a clear shot at him, but Curve was smart. He kept Kelee directly in front of him and out of his line of fire.

"I knew she'd bring yu' to me." Curve laughed dryly.

"She has no'ting to do with this," Sean insisted.

"Yu' 'tink she means more to yu' than my brother did to me?" Curve's tone was cold and chilling. Instantly Sean knew he meant to kill Kelee.

"Sean," Kelee cried, reaching out to him.

Curve intended to kill Kelee, Sean could see it in his eyes. Kelee's face was overcome with fear and it tore at his heart. Sean kept his eyes on her. He couldn't lose her, not like this. Kelee didn't deserve this. Sean looked at Curve and knew it had to end right here, right now. Curve laughed and tightened his hold on Kelee. Kelee's sobs tore a deeper hole into Sean's heart.

Kelee's heart was racing so fast she couldn't breathe. She had to take short quick breaths to remain conscious. Curve stank of cigar. The scent was overwhelming. His hold on her was starting to make her dizzy. Tears were streaming down her cheeks. Curve meant to kill her for Sean's killing his brother. Kelee didn't want to die, not like this.

"Jus' let her go, Curve, this is between me an' yu'," Sean said. Curve laughed again, his hot cigar-scented breath warming her cheek. Kelee shivered in fear.

"It's too bad she has to die," Curve said and Kelee's knees began to buckle. *Please, God, don't let me die,* Kelee prayed.

"No!" Sean shouted and rushed at them. Kelee watched in horror as Curve shot Sean. The impact sent him slamming against the wall. Kelee screamed. Curve let her go and she ran over to Sean. He lay facedown, motionless. She threw herself onto him. He couldn't be dead, not like this. Her heart exploded into a million pieces. She'd lost Sean.

"Sean, Sean, oh, God, no," she cried.

"Yu' made it so easy," Curve said above her.

Kelee looked up at him to see that he had his gun pointed at Sean's head.

"No," Kelee cried, covering Sean's body with hers.

"Jus' makin' sure he's dead," Curve said, getting ready to pull the trigger again.

Suddenly a voice came over a PA system. "THIS IS THE COAST GUARD. CURVE, COME OUT WITH YU' HANDS UP."

"Shit." Curve took off downstairs.

Kelee lay on top of Sean, crying. He'd sacrificed himself for her. It was so unfair; why did he have to die? Kelee heard Sean moan and move beneath her. He wasn't dead. She quickly turned him over. She didn't see any blood, but she saw the bullet hole in his shirt just under his chest. She felt his chest and realized that he had his bulletproof vest on. Sean opened his eyes, looking at her.

"Thank God," Kelee cried, excited and relieved, throwing her arms around his neck, kissing him all over his face.

"I'm good, jus' winded." He coughed and looked around. "Where is he?"

"The coast guard is here, he took off."

Sean started to get up but stumbled a bit. Kelee helped him to his feet. He leaned against the wall clutching his ribs where he'd been shot, catching his breath. Kelee saw his gun a few feet away and picked it up, handing it to him.

"Thanks." He took it and slapped a new clip in it without missing a beat.

"Come on." He took her hand and they headed downstairs. Kelee held his hand as tight as she could. There was no way she was letting go of him until she got off this damn island.

Downstairs Sean found Jack slumped in a corner, bleeding from a shoulder wound. He rushed over to him. He had a nasty hole in his shoulder.

"I'm good. Curve," he said through the pain and pointed at the back door.

"Tyce?"

Jack pointed to the other end of the room where Tyce lay facedown. "I took care of him, tried to pull a fast one on me. Curve's man shot me." Jack winced under the pain.

"So there are two of them?"

"Yeah." Jack winced.

The whine of the helicopter starting up could be heard.

"Kelee, stay with Jack," Sean said and headed out the back door.

Sean ran outside to see Curve getting into the helicopter. Curve paused as he was about to close the door. He looked at Sean, surprised, and instantly started firing at him with an M-16 rifle. Sean ducked back inside the house, bullets missing him by inches. No way in hell; he wasn't going to let Curve slip out of his hands, not this time.

"The crate," Jack shouted at him, pointing to the crate that was holding the back door open. When the firing stopped, Sean ran to the crate. He shot the lock off to see a handheld rocket launcher. He quickly pulled it out; it was loaded. Sean went back outside to see the helicopter taking off over the ocean. Sean flipped off the cap, lined up the helicopter and pressed the trigger. The blast of the rocket leaving the shell caused him to stumble; a sharp pain ignited in his chest where he'd been hit. For a moment it took his breath away. Sean watched in satisfaction as the missile connected with the helicopter and it exploded in a ball of fire, falling into the ocean in flaming pieces. Now it was finally over. Sean dropped the rocket launcher, no longer able to hold it. The pain was getting worse in his chest.

Six coast guards came running up to him moments later.

"Search every hole in that house," he told them. They nodded and ran into the house.

"Got him?" Jack asked, coming up to him with Kelee at his side. Sean looked at Jack, then at Kelee, grateful they were both alive. Kelee looked at him, concerned.

"Yeah, it's over," Sean said, rubbing his still stinging ribs where Curve's bullet had impacted and would have taken his life if he had not been wearing his vest. Kelee stared at him rubbing his ribs; he saw dread in her eyes. He gave her a reassuring smile, but it hurt like hell and he couldn't help wrenching under the pain. Instantly, Kelee was beside him.

"Yu' OK?"

"I think I broke a couple of ribs when I took that bullet," he moaned, leaning against her.

The coast guard helicopter set down not far from them and two guards jumped out and ran over to them. One assisted Jack and the other Sean into the helicopter. Kelee followed and was helped into the helicopter. A few minutes later they were air bound and heading back to St. Pala.

Sean slumped into the seat, trying to catch his breath; the pain was getting to him. He held his ribs. He opened his eyes to find Kelee staring at him. Once again the fear in her eyes unnerved him. He knew she'd gone through a lot in the past week and its effect on her was no doubt traumatic. She'd witnessed him kill a man today; he wondered how that made her feel. She would need time to process it all, but for now she was safe and she was unhurt, and that was all he cared about at that moment.

Kelee was in a daze staring at Sean. He had saved her life today by taking a bullet for her. If it hadn't been for his bulletproof vest she was sure he would have died. She wondered if he would have really died for her. In the short time she'd been here she'd been kidnapped and held hostage by a madman who would have killed her. It was all so much. Suddenly, she felt like she couldn't breathe, her head was starting to throb. She desperately wanted to see Lori; she was concerned about her condition and the stress it had caused. She prayed Lori, the baby, and Allan were OK.

"Did yu' see Lori, is she OK?" she asked Sean.

"The last time I saw her she was doing fine; a little shaken, but the doctors were still monitoring her."

"An' Allan?"

"Good; he wasn't hurt."

"Thank God." She sighed, closing her eyes. Kelee knew it was over but the fear was still with her.

"Every'ting is OK now. Yu' safe, there's no' ting for yu' to worry 'bout anymore," Sean told her. Kelee wished she could believe him. So much had happened to her in such a short time, all she wanted to do was get away from it all. It was just too much. Kelee pressed her lips together, holding back her tears.

Chapter 20

They were taken to the same hospital where Lori was. Jack was taken to surgery to remove the bullet from his arm and Sean was taken to x-ray to see how bad his ribs were. Kelee went to the nurse's station to find out if Lori was still admitted. The nurse told her that Lori had gone into premature labor and had given birth an hour ago. Kelee's heart raced with anticipation at seeing Lori and her new niece. Both Lori and the baby were doing fine. Kelee thanked God and raced to the room where Lori now was. She rushed into the room to see Lori sitting up in bed, breastfeeding. Allan was sitting at her bedside watching in awe.

"Kelee," Allan and Lori said in union.

Kelee ran over to her, throwing her arms around Lori and the baby, kissing her cheek. Tears welled up in her eyes.

"Thank God yu' OK." Lori started to cry. Kelee looked down at her adorable niece and kissed the top of the baby's bald head. She looked at Allan.

"Yu' OK?" she asked. The last time she had seen him he was unconscious. Allan touched the back of his head where he'd been hit and smiled.

"I'm good."

"I'm so sorry for everything." Kelee choked up.

"It's not yu' fault," Lori insisted.

"If I hadn't come here"—she brushed away the tears that were rolling down her cheeks—"yu', Allan, the baby, none of this would have happened." Kelee couldn't help but feel responsible for everything. If she hadn't gotten involved with Sean, none of this would have happened.

"Stop right there," Lori demanded. "None of this is yu' fault. I have a healthy baby, she came a little early, yes, but she's perfectly fine." Lori smiled down at the baby feeding at her breast. The baby was on the small side, but she was beautiful and feeding hungrily. Kelee caressed her small bald head and smiled.

"Where's Sean, is he OK?" Lori asked.

"He's in x-ray," Kelee told her.

"X-ray; why?"

"He was shot close range, but he was wearing his vest. I think he might have broken some ribs."

"Thank God it wasn't any worse," Lori said, relieved.

Allan got up and ushered Kelee into his seat. "I'm goin' to get some'ting to eat, an' check on Sean," he announced and left them alone.

"She has no hair," Lori moaned, caressing the baby's head.

"We were both bald when we were born, remember?" Kelee reminded her.

"Oh, yeah, we were." She smiled, caressing the baby's cheek. The baby opened her eyes; she had Allan's blue eyes. Kelee smiled as the baby grasped her finger.

"I want to hear every'ting that happened," Lori insisted. Kelee really didn't want to talk about it, but knowing Lori she wouldn't stop until she got the full story. Maybe if she did, then she would figure out how to solve her dilemma of dealing with Sean and the risk that came with being with him.

Sean was grateful to be out of x-ray. He was dying to see Kelee—he needed to make sure she was OK. He was given a painkiller and his ribs were bandaged. Three of his ribs had been broken and he had a nasty bruise. He found out that Lori was still in the hospital, having given birth. He was grateful to know she and the baby were doing fine. Jack was recovering, the bullet successfully removed from his shoulder. Jack was resting surrounded by his wife and kids when Sean stopped by to see him. Giving Jack time with his family, Sean went in search of Lori, knowing he'd find Kelee with her. He couldn't help but be worried about her. He didn't like the look of fear in her eyes in the chopper earlier. He needed to make sure she knew that she was safe now.

Kelee finished telling Lori what she had gone through. While she felt relieved it was all over, she couldn't help the dread feeling that had taken hold of her.

"Yu' safe now," Lori told her.

"I don't feel it," she confessed.

"I know it's hard after all yu've been through, but yu' can't let it consume yu'. Yu' don't have any'ting to be afraid of anymore."

"I know." She sighed, tired.

"Then what's really botherin' yu'?"

"I don't think I can be with him, not after what happened. I can't live with that kind of fear," she admitted with all honesty.

Lori looked at her, disappointed. "Don't yu' love him?"

Kelee looked at Lori, surprised by her question. "I think yu' seein' too much into what went on between Sean and me," Kelee told her.

"So yu' tellin' me yu' don't love him?"

"Love him, that's too much for me right now.

Plus, after what happened, I don't think I can be with a man like him. I can't always be lookin' over my shoulder wonderin' when some maniac who has a vendetta against him will target me."

"He loves yu', Kelee. He wouldn't let any'ting happen to yu'."

"It doesn't matter. I can't be with him. Plus, I didn't come here to find a man. I came here to be with yu' and the baby, and if I'd done that I wouldn't have ended up in Sean's drama. I just need to focus on what I came here to do and leave it at that." She smiled at her niece, who had fallen asleep.

"He wouldn't have gone through all he did to get yu' back if he didn't love yu'," Lori told her. Covering her breast, she placed the baby against her shoulder, tapping her back gently.

"Could we stop talkin' about Sean?"

"Why?"

"It's too complicated."

"It's not that complicated if yu' love him."

"I don't love him," she insisted. "And could yu' stop talking about Sean? I just want to forget everything that happened, everything, including him."

"I think yu' handlin' this all wrong," Lori said, disappointed. "Yu' two have such a strong bond, don't throw it away."

"We have nothing," Kelee said dryly. "And what we had I'd rather forget," she said with determination. She had come to a decision; she wanted nothing more to do with Sean St. John.

"Hey, man, how yu' feelin?" Kelee heard Allan ask just outside the door.

"Good," Sean's voice responded. Kelee spun around, looking at the door. Allan entered with a puzzled look on his face. When Sean didn't follow him, Kelee's stomach crunched up in fear.

"Was that Sean?" she asked, knowing it was him—she had heard his voice.

"Yes, wasn't he in here?"

"No, he never came in," Lori said.

"Funny, he was standing right at the door. I thought he was leavin'." Allan shrugged.

"He heard," Lori said.

"Oh, God." Kelee buried her face in her hands. She felt really bad. She never meant for him to hear anything she'd just said. She wanted to end it with him, but nicely.

Sean really couldn't blame Kelee for feeling the way she did. He'd put her through a lot. She'd been through a dramatic situation, being kidnapped and held hostage with a gun at her head. If she hated him for it all, he had no one to blame but himself. He'd lied to her and put her in danger. If she left St. Pala tomorrow he couldn't blame her. He didn't want to lose her, but she'd said it, she wanted to forget everything and that included him. Sean didn't feel like going home, so he decided to head west.

Lori was released from the hospital a few hours later and they all went home together. Lori hadn't bought up the subject of Sean and she was grateful. Back at the house Allan saw to Lori and the baby while Kelee retired to her room. She was emotionally and physically drained. Sean was all she could think of. She knew her words must have hurt him, but she just couldn't see herself with him knowing the danger that came with him. He was a good man and the chemistry was unbelievable between them, but she needed to feel safe; she knew she wouldn't be with him. She wished things had ended differently, but it was over and done now. There was nothing she could do about it. Tired, Kelee took a shower and get some much needed sleep.

When Kelee woke it was nine the next morning. She felt refreshed and her headache was gone. She found Lori in the living room watching the baby sleep in her bassinet. Kelee sat beside Lori looking at her niece.

"She's so beautiful," Kelee said, taking in the baby's small perfect features.

"Isn't she?" Lori beamed.

"Mama is going to be so happy when she sees her."

"Damn, I have to call her an' tell her I had the baby. Every'ting happened so fast I forgot to call her."

"Just don't tell her about me getting kidnapped. I don't think she needs to know all that."

"Yu' will tell her?" Lori asked.

"Yes, but not right now. There are other things I have to deal with first."

"Like Sean?"

"Like goin' back to my life in New York."

"Why don't yu' stay here?" Lori asked. Kelee looked at her. "St. Pala feels more like a home to yu' than New York, yu've said so yu'self. Wha' yu' have there besides work, which yu' can do here?"

Kelee did feel at home here. New York didn't feel this warm or welcoming to her. She knew it had to do with the fact that she didn't have any family there. She had family here, but her life and career were in New York not St. Pala.

"Stay with us," Lori said and hugged her. Kelee leaned against her.

"I can't. Not now," Kelee admitted. In her heart she wanted to stay but she couldn't. The thought of being in St. Pala and seeing Sean was too much. St. Pala was a small island and there was no way she could avoid him, he was like family to Lori and Allan.

"Go get some'ting to eat, yu' must be hungry,"

Lori told her. Kelee nodded and headed into the kitchen to get breakfast. A few minutes later Lori joined her, baby monitor in hand.

"I was thinkin'," Lori started. Kelee took a sip of her tea, ready for an earful.

"Go on," Kelee said.

"I think yu' should call Sean."

"I told yu' I don't want to have anything to do with him."

"After what he overheard, yu' need to clear the air with him. Tell him why yu' feel the way yu' do. Don't go back to New York without clearing 'tings up."

"I thought about that, but what difference would that make?"

"Sean is like family. I hate to see 'tings end badly between yu' two, that's all."

Kelee knew she was right, she had to talk to Sean, clear the air between them.

"Yu' right," Kelee admitted. Lori smiled with satisfaction. Kelee prayed Sean would want to talk to her after what he had overheard.

Sean wasn't at the house when Kelee called and his cell phone kept going straight to voice mail. Kelee called Jack, who was home recovering from his gunshot wound. Jack told her he'd give Sean a call. Two hours later Jack called back.

"Did yu' get him?" Kelee asked, anxious.

"Yeah," Jack said.

"Is he OK?" she asked.

"He didn't sound like himself," Jack told her.

"Did yu' tell him I wanted to talk to him?"

"Yes. He said it was over between yu' two. What happened?"

"He overheard some things that I didn't mean for him to hear. I just need to clear things up with him before I leave."

"When yu' leavin'?"

"Soon," she said. "Do yu' know where he is?"

"The cabin. He goes there to cool off when he's upset."

"Thank yu' and take care," Kelee told Jack.

"Yu' too."

Kelee found Jack and Lori in the living room. Lori was breastfeeding. Allan sat by her side, the baby holding onto his finger. There was so much love in his eyes for his daughter. A part of her envied what they had, a loving relationship and a beautiful baby.

"Did yu' get him?" Lori asked, looking up at her.

"Jack said he's at the cabin," Kelee told her, sitting across from them.

"I'll take yu' there if yu' like," Allan said. Kelee smiled at him, relieved.

"Sounds good to me." Lori beamed.

"Yu' want to pack a bag just in case?" Allan asked. Kelee smiled at him.

* * *

Sean sat on the beach under a coconut tree, staring out into the calm, crystal blue waters. It was a peaceful soothing sight and he wished his emotions were as such. Kelee's words kept replaying in his head. She couldn't be with a man like him because she feared for her life. She wanted to forget everything, including him. It hurt to know she felt that way. Yet he had no one but himself to blame; he had put her in danger and almost gotten her killed. He wasn't sure how he could take her fears away. He loved her and he wanted her in the worst way, but he also loved his work. He made a difference here. Because of him, crime was down and tourism was up in St. Pala. The people of St. Pala needed him, but he also needed Kelee; only she wanted nothing to do with him because of his work. So why did she want to talk to him? He wanted to see her, he missed her. He wanted to take her fears away, but he wasn't sure how anymore. He thought of calling her but he stopped himself. He needed time to clear his head, and then he could better deal with her if she still wanted to talk to him.

Less than half an hour later with an overnight bag in tow, Kelee kissed Lori and the baby on her way out. A few minutes later Allan and

Kelee headed towards View Coast. Kelee was a bundle of nerves.

"It's goin' to work out," Allan reassured her.

"I just don't want him hating me."

"Trust me, he doesn't. He's too crazy 'bout yu' to hate yu'."

"I need to make him understood, that's all." She chewed on her bottom lip.

"Yu' love him, right?"

Kelee suddenly realized that she was afraid of acknowledging her feelings for Sean.

"Yu' do love him?" Allan asked again.

"I haven't thought about that," she lied.

"Yu' don't 'tink 'bout love, yu' either in love or yu' not. So which one is it?" Allan pressed for an answer.

"I'm afraid to think about it," she admitted.

"Don't 'tink too hard an' lose him. He's a good man. Plus, Lori and I 'tink yu' two belong together."

Kelee couldn't help the smile that touched her lips. "Yu' do?"

"Sure, an' yu' stayin' in St. Pala would mean the world to Lori," Allan added.

"Oh, so this is about me staying in St. Pala?"

"Partially. But seriously, I know Sean an' when I tell yu' he loves yu', he does."

"Did he tell yu' that?" Kelee asked, curious.

"No, he didn't have to; anyone can see it when he looks at yu'."

For the rest of the ride Kelee sat in quiet reflection wondering if Sean really did love her. She knew ten years ago they had made a connection, but she didn't know how he really felt about her now. He had proved to her that he would have given his life to rescue her. She wondered how much further it went. She knew she felt a great deal for it, but she was afraid to admit it in fear that he didn't return her feelings. She wasn't sure what she'd say to him upon seeing him, but she had to get it all out in the open.

They arrived at the cabin and Kelee couldn't bring herself to get out of the car. Fear had gripped her; there was no turning back if she walked into that cabin. This was it; she would have to face what she felt for Sean and it scared her to death.

"Want me to check if he's there?" Allan asked.

Kelee looked at him, snapping out of her spell. "No, no. I got this, thanks." She kissed Allan's cheek and got out of the car, pulling her bag from the backseat.

Kelee walked up to the door of the cabin, her heart racing. This was it. She stared at the door. This was the place that they had started and this would be the place they would either continue or end. She glanced back to see Allan still waiting in the car. She took a deep breath and knocked twice. She heard footsteps and the door opened. He stood before her in loose sweatpants and nothing else. He looked tired, but still fine. She saw the round bruise on his side where he'd been shot. Again she thanked God he was alive, that he'd only walked away with a few broken ribs.

Sean stared at her in disbelief. He looked down at the bag in her hand, then outside. He looked back at her and pulled her into the cabin, slamming the door.

Instantly she was in his arms. His mouth engulfed hers in a heated kiss. The kiss they shared seemed to last forever, neither wanting to end it or let go of each other. Kelee's heart was racing so fast she had to take a deep breath when the kiss ended. Sean was gazing at her with such intensity for a moment she couldn't speak.

"I never meant to hurt yu' with what I said. I didn't mean it that way." She found her voice.

"Yu' showin' up here says as much." He smiled down at her, caressing her cheek.

"I wanted yu' to know that I don't hate yu', I don't hate anything that happened between us. It's jus' that when I think of what yu' do, it scares me to death. I just didn't know how to handle it."

"I know, but yu' must understand that it's not always like that. Goin' after Curve was dangerous, but otherwise my work never gets that dangerous."

"It doesn't?"

"No; I can't even remember the last time I had to use my gun. I usually let the police handle the raids and busts, but when he targeted yu' I jus' couldn't leave it up to them. Yu' mean too much to me, Kelee. I'm sorry yu' had to go through any of that, I really am. But there's no reason to be afraid anymore."

He kissed her gently, soothing all her fears. Kelee clung to him, never wanting to let him go. He hugged her close.

"Yu' scare me, Sean," she told him.

"Why?" he asked, confused and hurt.

"Yu' make me feel things, things that I am afraid to admit to."

"An' now?" he asked with a slight smile.

"I'm not afraid anymore." She smiled, kissing him with all her heart.

They kissed and undressed each other with an intense urgency. Sean took her, naked and in his arms, into the bedroom. He placed her in the middle of the bed, covering her body with his. In one swift move he was inside her, loving her.

"I love yu'," she whispered against his lips. He stopped and looked down at her.

"Yu' know how long I've waited to hear yu' say that?" he asked.

"Ten years." She grinned, moving beneath him. He smiled and kissed her deeply. She didn't want him to ever stop making love to her, or loving her.

"I love yu'," he told her, caressing her lips with his tongue. Her heart rejoiced at his words. She moaned, loving him all over again, loving him forever.